The spider's web

Author: Williams, Laura E
Reading Level: 4.1 UG
Point Value: 4.0
ACCELERATED READER QUIZ# 31419

THE SPIDER'S WEB

ALSO BY LAURA E. WILLIAMS

Behind the Bedroom Wall

The Long Silk Strand

THE SPIDER'S WEB

LAURA E. WILLIAMS

ERICA MAGNUS, ILLUSTRATOR

MILKWEED
EDITIONS

© 1999, Text by Laura E. Williams
© 1999, Illustrations by Erica Magnus
Milkweed Editions, 430 First Avenue North, Minneapolis, MN 55401. http://www.milkweed.org
Distributed by Publishers Group West

Published 1999 by Milkweed Editions
Printed in the United States of America
Cover design by Sarah Purdy
Cover painting and interior illustrations by Erica Magnus
Interior design by Donna Burch
The text of this book is set in Sabon.
   99 00 01 02 03   5 4 3 2 1
First Edition

Milkweed Editions is a not-for-profit publisher. This book has been underwritten by the Righteous Persons Foundation. We also gratefully acknowledge support of Alliance for Reading Funders: Cray Research, a Silicon Graphics Company; Dayton Hudson Circle of Giving; Ecolab Foundation; Musser Fund; Jay and Rose Phillips Foundation; Rathmann Family Foundation; Target Stores; United Arts School and Partnership Funds. Other support has been provided by the Elmer L. and Eleanor J. Andersen Foundation; James Ford Bell Foundation; Dayton's, Mervyn's, and Target Stores by the Dayton Hudson Foundation; Doherty, Rumble & Butler Foundation; Dorsey & Whitney Foundation; General Mills Foundation; Honeywell Foundation; Jerome Foundation; McKnight Foundation; Minnesota State Arts Board through an appropriation by the Minnesota State Legislature; Norwest Foundation on behalf of Norwest Bank Minnesota, Norwest Investment Management & Trust, Lowry Hill, Norwest Investment Services, Inc.; Lawrence and Elizabeth Ann O'Shaughnessy Charitable Income Trust in honor of Lawrence M. O'Shaughnessy; Oswald Family Foundation; Piper Jaffray Companies, Inc.; Ritz Foundation on behalf of Mr. and Mrs. E. J. Phelps Jr.; John and Beverly Rollwagen Fund of the Minneapolis Foundation; St. Paul Companies, Inc.; Star Tribune Foundation; and generous individuals.

Library of Congress Cataloging-in-Publication Data
Williams, Laura E.
     The spider's web / Laura E. Williams, [text] and illustrator. — 1st ed.
       p.   cm.
     Summary: Lexi's unhappy home life with an alcoholic mother drives her to join a neo-Nazi group, but eventually she discovers that her new friends thrive on hatred and destruction.
       ISBN 1-57131-621-3 (cloth). — ISBN 1-57131-622-1 (pbk)
       [1. Neo-Nazism—Fiction. 2. Alcoholism—Fiction.] I. Title.
PZ7.W666584Sp   1999
[Fic]—dc21   98-32218
                                                           CIP
                                                            AC

This book is dedicated with love to my sister,
Sue McCarthy Henneberry, and to my brothers,
Tim Williams and Mark Williams.
And to children everywhere, who need to know
that not all the paths in life are clearly marked,
and even the ones that are marked
are sometimes treacherous.

Special thanks go to the following people
for their help in shaping this novel:
  Haia Spiegel
  Debby Rossman
  Pegi Deitz Shea
  Grace LaMell
  Janice Ryskiewicz Reineke
  Sally Williams
  Patti Lippman Axsom
  My RWA critique group
  my agent, Edy Selman
  Emilie Buchwald and all the wonderful
  people at Milkweed Editions

I'd like to emphasize that the main characters
in this novel are completely fictitious and bear no
resemblance to any known persons, living or
deceased.

THE SPIDER'S WEB

CHAPTER ONE

GASPING FOR BREATH, she crouched behind a scraggly bush. Her lungs ached. She hadn't run so fast or so long since she'd been on the track team two years ago. And a lot had happened since then. For one thing, she didn't run track anymore. Her dad had been the only one who cared about her being on the team, and since he hadn't cared enough to stick around . . .

Trying to hold her breath so she could hear better, Lexi Jordan listened for her pursuers. A dog howled down the street. The bass from someone's stereo thumped the air from an open window, but no pounding footsteps raced toward her. She must have lost them at last.

Cautiously, she stood up. She had to keep going or she'd be late. Trying to move swiftly and quietly, she hurried down the sidewalk, keeping to the nighttime shadows as much as possible.

She flung her left arm to the side, ditching the evidence she'd clutched in her hand as she'd run away. A can of red spray paint. Red for blood. The empty container hit a stone, then tumbled into the darkness. She winced at the noise. To her it sounded like a gunshot on the quiet street.

"I think one of them went this way," a man shouted. "Come on!"

Lexi froze. They were still after her. Pulling the drawstrings of her navy sweatshirt hood tighter around her face, she edged quickly toward a house, as far away from the glow of the streetlight as possible. She could just make out the steam, like cigarette smoke, billowing out of her mouth with each breath she took.

Three dark forms hurried down the street, peering into shadows and hedges, moving closer and closer. In a couple of minutes they would stumble over her.

One stopped and nosed in a bush, like a dog following a scent. When he stood up, he held the spray paint can gingerly between two fingers. "Look what I found. Evidence!"

Sweat slicked Lexi's palms. Now they had the can with her fingerprints all over it. If they caught her, there would be no way out of it.

She looked around. The only place to hide was a dark porch to her left. But first, she'd have to cross the lighted driveway.

The men came closer.

She had no choice.

Taking a deep breath, she darted across the driveway

and bounded up the three front stairs in her heavy boots. The Doc Martens clomped on the wood as she crossed the porch, even though she tried to lighten her steps.

She huddled in the far corner, behind a hanging swing. Her heart thumped in her ears, and her breath rasped through slightly parted lips.

Less than one hour ago, what she was going to do had seemed like a good idea. "Easy," Mick had promised. "No sweat," Devon had assured her. But now she was on the run. She couldn't get caught. Her mother would ground her for sure. But, more important, Mick and the others were depending on her, and she couldn't let them down.

Lexi peered through the slats of the swing as the dark figures crossed the driveway.

"They got away," one man said. "But at least we have this." He shook the can and the ball inside rattled.

"Damn kids," another said. "Let's look down the rest of this street and then go around the block and back to the temple. Maybe we'll get lucky."

Lexi sighed with relief. None of her friends had been caught.

She forced herself to count to one hundred before she stood. Her left leg had cramped up, and she had to massage it for a minute before she could even take a step.

She was so intent on walking quietly across the porch, planning on disappearing silently into the night and heading for the rendezvous, that she didn't notice the door open until a woman's sharp voice cut across her nerves.

"Who are you?" the voice demanded. At the same time, the porch light flashed on.

Lexi whirled around. "I . . . oh man, you scared me!" she blurted out, shielding her eyes against the sudden light. A shadowy form that looked like a smudged charcoal drawing stood on the other side of a screen door.

"What are you doing here? Who are you?" the woman's voice insisted, only the *what* sounded more like *vaht*.

Lexi glanced toward the street, afraid the high-pitched voice would bring back her pursuers.

"Some guys are chasing me," Lexi said, tugging on the drawstrings that dangled under her chin. "I ran up here to hide from them. I . . . I don't know what they'll do to me if they catch me." That was all true.

For a moment the woman said nothing. Lexi half expected her to scream. Instead, she opened the screen door and motioned to Lexi. "Come in," she said.

Lexi stared.

"Hurry up, before they find you, those ruffians." The woman moved aside to give Lexi room to enter. "Used to be this neighborhood was quiet and safe. Now, ach!"

Lexi slipped into the house. It wouldn't hurt to stay out of view a little longer.

The woman closed the screen door. Before she closed the front door, she peered up and down the street.

Appearing satisfied, she firmly shut the door and turned, rubbing her hands against her sweatered arms. Her gray hair, which she'd braided, was wrapped around her head like a tidy coil of rope. Her wrinkled face looked like a topographical map, her eyes twin lakes of blue on either side of a steep mountain.

"Are you cold?" the old woman asked. "It's chilly outside."

Lexi shook her head. Adrenaline was keeping her warm.

The woman suddenly stepped forward and exclaimed, "You're bleeding!"

Lexi jerked her hand up to look at it, then shoved it into her pocket. It wasn't blood, but red spray paint that the woman had seen on her fingers and the cuff of her sweatshirt.

"It's nothing," Lexi said.

The woman pursed her lips as if she didn't believe Lexi. She motioned toward the phone. "Would you like to call someone to pick you up? It's late."

Again, Lexi shook her head. The woman frowned. "Your parents let you out so late on a school night? Alone?"

"I don't have *parents,*" she said. Now that her dad was gone, she only had one *parent,* but she wasn't going to explain that to this lady.

"Ah," the woman said, nodding.

Ah? What did that mean? Lexi looked away, hoping

to stop any more questions. She glanced around the room. It was small, crammed full of bookcases over-crowded with books and picture frames and little statues of elephants. Lace doilies covered the tables. In the far corner sat an overstuffed chair under a floor lamp. A book lay open across the armrest.

The walls were crowded with more photos, many of them black-and-white, of people wearing old-fashioned clothes. Lexi leaned forward to examine one of the faded photos more closely. It was a picture of a young girl, about the age her sister was now, maybe nine or ten, standing between two adults. None of them was smiling.

Lexi wondered if the girl in the photo was the old lady when she'd been a kid, and she mentally compared that photo to the one of her family that sat on the mantle at home. It was an "AD" photo. After Divorce. Everyone in that picture was smiling. At least they *looked* happy. Mom had said she'd smack them if they didn't smile for the camera.

The BD photos—Before Divorce—the ones with the real smiles, Mom had shoved into bottom drawers and dumped in cardboard boxes in the attic.

"What's your name?" the woman asked, breaking into Lexi's thoughts. She lifted a hand to pat her neat hair.

Lexi hesitated, looking at the wooden floor, old and worn but still glossy. "Amy," she said.

"I'm Mrs. Zeidler. Ursula Zeidler. Used to be people called older people by their last names, but nowadays . . ." She shrugged. "You may call me whatever you like."

Lexi looked at her and smiled stiffly, nodding politely as she had been trained to do. Then she looked away. Pretty soon she'd leave and never see this old lady again. She didn't need to know her name. Moving to the window, she brushed aside the wispy curtain and looked out, but she couldn't see anything except her own reflection in the glass. "I think I'll go now. They must be gone."

The woman shook her head. "Just wait a few more minutes. It's so dark. It's better to be safe." She paused. "Are you sure you don't want to call someone?"

Lexi shrugged. "Don't worry, I'll be fine. I really don't live that far away."

"Oh? Where do you live?"

"On Rockhaven Drive." Lexi bit her tongue. Why had she told the truth?

"Ah, that's a nice neighborhood."

"It's okay." Lexi shifted restlessly. Her adrenaline high was fizzling away in the heat of the room. She loosened her hood. The old lady must have had the heat cranked to 105 degrees. She needed some cold fall air to wake her up and get her blood pumping.

Mrs. whatever-her-name-was just stood there, clasping her hands together. Her fingers looked soft and doughy like Nanna's had. Lexi suddenly had the urge to take the woman's hands in her own, the way she used to take Nanna's and make her play ring-around-the-rosy.

Shaking away the impulse, Lexi felt a drop of sweat trickle down her scalp. It was way too hot in here. She moved toward the door. "I really have to go."

The woman looked out the window, holding the curtain aside, shading her eyes against the reflecting glare of the lamp. "Everything looks quiet—"

"Good. Gotta go." Lexi turned the knob on the front door and pulled it. As the door swung open, a wind whipped through the outer screen door, blowing the hood off her head. Her sweaty scalp, shaved bare, prickled in the sudden blast of cold.

Lexi moved to flip the hood back up over her head, but it was too late. She could tell by the shocked look on the old lady's face that she had seen the tattoo above her left ear. The tattoo took up nearly the whole side of her scalp. Hard to miss.

"I call it my spider," Lexi explained, even though the woman hadn't asked. "It's my good luck charm. It keeps me safe."

The woman didn't say anything. She just kept staring.

CHAPTER TWO

As URSULA STARED AT THE black marks, the years seemed to melt away. *Once again she was a girl. She held the flaming torch high, even though her arm ached, her back ached, and her feet pinched in her too-tight boots.* "Sieg Heil! Sieg Heil!" *she shouted out along with her comrades as she stared at the red flag with the bold, black, spiderlike swastika twisting in the middle of it. Her heart swelled with pride.* "Heil Hitler! Heil Hitler!"

The cry echoed down the street. Ursula knew she was just one light among thousands of others, marching in this torch parade, but even so, her light counted.

All the torches together lit up the night sky, giving the features of everyone nearby a fiery glow, as though they had been dipped in liquid gold.

She glanced at her best friend, marching beside her. They grinned at each other.

"Do you think we'll get to see him?" Hildegard asked in an undertone.

Ursula's heart thumped at the thought of seeing her Führer. "I don't know."

Hildegard sighed. "If only I could see him, then I'd have something to brag about to Wolfgang. He thinks he's wonderful just because he's one second older than I am."

Ursula laughed. "And a lot taller, too."

"But stupider."

Ursula would have laughed some more, but their troop leader was glaring at them. Ursula composed her face and stared straight ahead like the rest of her Jungmädel comrades.

The heavy clop, clop of their shoes beat right into her heart, until she was sure her heart was pounding at the same pace. She kept her face still, but her eyes looked around. It was the goal of everyone on parade to actually catch a glimpse of Adolf Hitler, their wonderful leader. Who would be the lucky ones?

The march seemed to go on for hours and hours. At last they passed the stand where Hitler stood watching. Ursula felt the ripple of excitement pass through the marchers as they stomped by the raised platform.

She didn't dare turn her head, or even let her eyes flicker to the side. A good German was strong and disciplined. And she was a good German. Her job right now was to carry her torch and march on for however long it took to conquer the world.

But at the last second, the urge became too much. Her gaze shot to the side, then returned to the correct forward position. It took a moment for her brain to catch up with what she had seen. Or what she thought she had seen. No, she corrected herself. She had seen *him. Adolf Hitler. She'd recognize his mustache and regal bearing anywhere. She had actually seen him!*

She couldn't wait for the parade to be over. She had to tell Hildegard. Had Hildegard seen him, too? She didn't dare glance at her friend while they were marching so close to the Führer. It was especially important now to be on her best behavior.

At last the parade ended. Her Jungmädel *group gathered around, talking excitedly about the night as the leaders collected the torches. A few girls whispered that they had seen the Führer. If a leader heard, they might get in trouble for not looking straight ahead the way they were supposed to.*

Ursula tugged on Hildegard's sleeve. "I saw him!" she said in a hushed voice. "I really did!"

Hildegard turned to her, her eyes wide. "Really? What did he look like?"

Ursula laughed. "Like he always does, silly. Like he does in all the photos we have of him from the paper."

Hildegard stuck out her lower lip. "I wanted to see him, too, but I was afraid to look."

Just then, Wolfgang charged over, calling their names. He had the same straight brown hair as his sister.

When he got close, he grinned and puffed out his chest. "See anything interesting during the parade?"

Ursula nodded. "I saw the Führer!"

Wolfgang's chest deflated a bit. He turned to his twin sister. "Did you?"

She shook her head. That perked him up a bit. "Well, I did. I stared at him. I think he saw me."

Hildegard rolled her eyes. "If he did, he'll probably report you to your troop leader for not looking where you were supposed to, Dummkopf!"

Wolfgang poked his sister in the stomach. "You're jealous!" Then he ran off with his friends.

"He thinks he's so heroic," Hildegard said with a huff. "I'll show him who's heroic."

"How?" Ursula had heard all this before.

The girls started walking with the flow of people. The parade was over and it was time to head home. Now that the excitement was dying down, the air felt colder. Summer was definitely gone.

"I don't know yet," Hildegard said after a moment. "But I'll think of something."

Ursula just shrugged. Her best friend was always competing with her twin. But it was Wolfgang who usually won.

Ursula and Hildegard had been friends since they were babies. They lived across the street from each other and became best friends when they joined the same Jungmädel group. Now they did almost everything together.

As they neared their street, the crowds had thinned out considerably. By the time they turned onto their short, cobbled road, there were very few people on the sidewalks.

They stopped in front of Ursula's house.

"I'll meet you tomorrow before school," Hildegard said.

"Don't be late."

Hildegard held out her hands. "Me? Late?"

Ursula groaned and giggled at the same time. She was just about to turn away and go into her house

15

when a flickering light caught her attention. Most houses along the street were dark or had a single light on in one of the bedrooms or in the front room. But this light was different—weaker, flickering like the light from a candle. Suddenly the light disappeared.

"What's wrong?" Hildegard asked, looking over her shoulder.

Ursula shrugged. "I thought I saw a light behind that window. She pointed across the street to the house next to Hildegard's. It was the Reineke's house.

Hildegard turned to look. "I don't see anything."

"It's gone now. Or maybe I just imagined it. I'm tired from marching, and that torch was heavy."

They both stared at the house a moment longer. One window glowed behind a heavy curtain, but there was no light in the high window under the peak of the roof. It was dark and it stayed dark, a single, blind eye.

"I'm going in," Ursula finally said, shivering with cold. "Heil Hitler."

Hildegard absently waved and crossed the street to her own house. When Ursula looked back just before shutting her front door, she saw Hildegard still staring up at the Reineke's house.

Slowly, Ursula's memories receded, and once again she was an old woman, staring at the four crooked legs of the swastika on the girl's head.

The girl was smiling at her, but Ursula saw that hers wasn't a happy face. For one thing, Amy was too thin.

The skin stretched too tight, pushing out the cheek-bones. And the blue-black swastika sat like a deadly spider above her ear.

"Is that thing painted on?" Ursula couldn't help the wobble in her voice.

"It's a tattoo," the girl said. "It's *permanent*. What's the matter? Don't you like it?"

Ursula's heart pounded. "Why do you have that evil thing there?"

"It's not evil." She lifted her right fist at a forty-five degree angle. "It's power!"

Ursula took a shuddering breath. She retreated until her chair pressed against the back of her knees. "No, it's not."

The sneer on the girl's face reminded Ursula of someone, but at the moment she couldn't think of whom. She eased down onto her chair, her arthritis screaming in her joints.

The girl watched her through slitted eyes. "You're just an old lady. What do you know about the Aran race?"

"Aran?" Ursula repeated, though she knew what the girl meant.

"Yeah, the white race. The strongest race. We're going to rule the world," she said. She flipped the hood up over her head, hiding the swastika.

"It's Aryan, not Aran," Ursula whispered.

"What did you say?"

Ursula shook her head. "Nothing," she said a bit louder.

"Anyway," the girl continued, "we're going to get rid of all the bla—niggers and—and spicks and kikes and people like that."

"How?"

"Scare them away. Mick says they should go back to where they came from, like Africa and Mexico."

"And what's so wonderful about being white?"

"White is might! White is right!" the girl said, flashing the Nazi salute.

"Why?"

"We're smarter and . . . and stuff like that."

The whooshing sound in her ears, Ursula knew, was blood rushing to her head. She put a hand over her heart, trying to soothe the heavy thumping. "You don't know what you're talking about," she choked out. "The stupidity of your words! Why you—"

"What do you know?" The sneer was wavering.

"I know too much!" Ursula cried out. *I was one of Hitler's children!*"

"What?"

"I believed and I followed him before I knew . . . before I realized . . . before I understood . . ." Her voice trailed off. Her lips trembled and she willed herself not to cry. She would not cry. Not in front of this girl.

"What are you talking about?" the girl demanded. "I don't—"

"I think you'd better go now," Ursula said, cutting her off. Using the armrests of her chair, she pushed herself up and marched to the door, ignoring her tired, stiff muscles.

"Hey, I wanted to leave a long time ago," Lexi said. She shoved the screen door open. Just before slipping out, she paused and turned to face Ursula. She raised her right hand in a salute. *"Heil Hitler!"* she said. Then she disappeared into the dark, a ghostly shadow.

Ursula gathered her last burst of energy and slammed the door shut.

CHAPTER THREE

L EXI SLID THROUGH THE shadows. Glancing
at her Indiglo, she saw that it was almost ten. She
was late for the rendezvous at the Big Tree. She hesitated—maybe she should just go home.

At the corner, she paused. Left would take her into
the woods that surrounded the cemetery. Right would
take her home. Her mother probably hadn't even noticed she was gone. Not if she had a *business associate*
over. And her younger sister was probably asleep. She
turned left.

She pictured the woman she had just left. She felt almost sorry for her, standing there with that shocked expression on her face when she had seen her tattoo. But it
was just a swastika. Just a pattern. Everyone acted like
it was some big crime or terrible thing. At school, some
kids thought it was cool, others gave her dirty looks.
But what did she care? Mick and the others had praised
her and said that getting it done showed her loyalty, and
they had all treated her like she was their sister, like
family.

Lexi chanted to herself as she marched along, "White is might! White is right!" The old lady's question came back to her. *Why?* She had asked Mick that once, and he had yelled, "Because it is!" That was the only time he'd raised his voice to her. Told her not to ask any more stupid questions.

On West Road the streetlights were dimmer and farther apart. Dark crowded her on all sides. She couldn't help thinking the long rows of bumpy hedges looked like giant worms, and the occasional picket fences poked out of the ground like neat rows of bones. She shivered, chanting quietly again, "White is might! White is right!" Somehow she felt better, hearing her voice fill up the darkness.

When she got to a path worn into the lawn just past the water tower, she followed it. Mr. Johnson had given up a long time ago trying to keep kids from cutting across his property to get to Crocker's Woods.

Eventually she came to a chain-link fence that ran along the back of Johnson's land. Someone had probably taken pliers to it a long time ago, ripping a big gash. She ducked through the hole and made her way down the path. She saw only shadows under the cover of the trees. Here, there were no streetlights to give any illumination. Only the occasional sprinkle of moonlight lit the way.

She hated the dark. When Lexi was a little kid, her mom let her sleep with a night-light on and the hall door open. Even then it was easy to imagine monsters hiding under the bed, ready to nibble at her toes if she let them slip over the edge. How many times had she called out for someone to come save her from the bogeyman? And her mother had always come running, ready to wrap her in warm arms and hug away all her fears.

Lexi stepped over a large log blocking the path. Only it didn't look like a log, it looked like a crouching beast. She quickened her pace. She couldn't call out to her mother for help now. Besides, her mother had stopped running to her side a long time ago.

When she reached the Y, she moved off the main path and headed down a narrow trail that twisted and turned. At one point she wasn't even sure she was still on the path, but then she heard voices up ahead.

With relief, she stepped into the clearing by the Big Tree. Five heads swiveled in her direction, faces lit by the small fire burning in the middle of the ring.

"Here she is!" Devon cheered in his cracking voice.

Lexi smiled at her friend. He always made her feel welcome.

Mick held a stick in one hand, stabbing at the embers with it, a half-empty beer bottle in the other. He was the leader. He looked up at her and grinned. "What took you so long? Did you get lost?"

Lexi slipped forward and crouched down in the circle into a space Devon made for her. "I had to hide. I almost got caught."

Mick flashed her a look. "I'm glad you didn't."

Devon put a skinny arm over her shoulders. "Of course she didn't get caught. She's too smart for that."

Serge glared at her from across the fire. "What did you do with your spray can?"

"I . . . I tossed it. In the bushes."

"Jeez!" he exclaimed, throwing his empty bottle into the fire. A swarm of sparks erupted from the flames. "Didn't you think that maybe someone might find it and get your fingerprints off it?"

Lexi glared back at the bulky shape. He was new to their group. Came from some city out west. She hated the fact that he thought he knew everything.

"It's not like the police have my prints on file or anything," she argued.

Serge opened his mouth and puffed out his chest like he was going to explode, but Mick elbowed him in the ribs.

"Whatever," Serge grumbled, grabbing another beer out of a brown paper bag. "You guys are just hicks. You don't know what it means to be a *real* skin."

"But I'm sure he'll show us," Devon whispered to Lexi.

Lexi smiled back. Serge was always trying to boss them around, even though Mick was the leader.

"Plus," Serge continued, still aiming his beady eyes at her, "she's too young. She's just a punk and she'll get us all in trouble."

"But," Devon protested, "she's the same age as me, and—"

Mick held up his hand for silence. "Look, we already decided we need some younger recruits. The younger ones are easier to . . ." He glanced at Lexi and didn't finish his sentence. "Anyway, leave her alone."

Devon squeezed her shoulder. His breath smelled of alcohol. "Don't worry about it, Lexi. We know you won't screw up."

Lexi smiled gratefully at him. Serge usually left her alone, but lately he'd been acting like he didn't want her around anymore. She'd have to be extra careful. This was the first time they'd actually let her do any of the spraying. Usually she was only a lookout, but Mick said she'd been loyal and deserved to do more. She didn't want to disappoint him. If she made a mistake, maybe he wouldn't let her hang out with them.

She looked around the fire. No one was watching her except Serge with his small, too-close-together eyes. Karen's nose ring glinted in the flickering light like a golden tear. Beside Karen sat Mick. She felt safe in the circle with Devon on one side of her and Billy on the other, the darkness at their backs.

"Hey," Mick said, "I thought you told me your younger sister wanted to join us. Why don't you bring her along?"

Lexi shrugged, a little uneasy. How could she tell her friends that she didn't really want Shelby to be a skin?

She loved these guys. They were like family—better, even—but Shel was too young and Lexi didn't want her to get into trouble. Not that they did anything that bad—just spraypainting buildings and sometimes tumbling gravestones. It wasn't like they really hurt anyone, but still . . .

"Lexi?" Mick said.

"Oh, yeah, sure. Maybe next time."

"We all set for Thursday night?" Devon asked, looking at Mick.

Thankful for the change of subject, Lexi let out the breath she had been holding.

The leader nodded. "I am. Are you guys?" He looked around the circle. Everyone nodded.

The big night. Mick said it would show everyone who ruled. The idea had actually been Serge's, but Mick had quickly agreed and made up the plans.

"I don't know if I can sneak out," Lexi said.

All eyes turned to her. Immediately she wished she had kept her mouth shut.

Serge snorted with disgust. "I told you she was just a baby."

Mick silenced him with an abrupt hand gesture. "If you really want to be one of the chosen ones," he said softly, "you'll be there. We're counting on you. All of us."

Devon passed her a beer. "She won't let us down. Will you?"

Lexi shook her head as wings of nervousness fluttered in her stomach. She didn't really like to think about Thursday night, but she had no choice, not if she wanted to be accepted. She had shaved and tattooed her head to prove her loyalty, but that wasn't enough.

"Where did you hide tonight?" Serge asked.

The question shook Lexi out of her thoughts. She took a sip of the warm beer and passed it back to Devon. "On a porch. This old lady's house."

"Did she see you?"

Lexi's eyes flicked around at the Pack. Mick had come up with that name for their group, saying they were like a pack of white wolves out to protect their territory. Now they were all looking at her.

"Uh, yeah," she admitted.

Serge smacked his fist against his leg. "I knew it! I knew we couldn't trust her."

"I didn't tell her anything," Lexi protested.

Mick stopped jabbing the fire. "You mean you actually talked to her?"

Lexi swallowed hard. She didn't want to be kicked out of the Pack. She'd been hanging with them since last spring. Since the divorce. They were like family now. Better than family. Better than *her* family, anyway. Especially Devon. He really looked after her like a brother. She'd found a place where she actually belonged. For the first time in a long time, she felt special.

"I didn't tell her anything," she said.

"A lot of niggers live on Parker Street," Devon said with a scowl. "Was she a blackie?"

"No. She . . . she even told me she was one of Hitler's children!" Lexi blurted out.

Only the sound of sticks popping in the fire broke the silence as they all stared at her.

"One of Hitler's children?" Serge repeated a moment later, his voice charged with excitement.

Devon looked confused. "Hitler didn't have no children, did he?"

Serge laughed. "Not one of his kids, you idiot, she meant she was in Hitler's youth group. She's a Nazi!"

"Cool," Karen said, her thin fingers fluttering up to touch her nose ring. "A real, old-fashioned Nazi."

Lexi realized the accent she'd heard was a German one.

"Hey, maybe she knew Hitler," Billy said in his deep voice. At almost fifteen, he was only one year older than Lexi and Devon, but Devon sounded a lot younger with his voice constantly cracking. No one teased him about it since he'd tackled Serge for making a puberty joke at his expense. Serge had swiped him away like a fly.

Now Serge grinned. "Let's go ask her."

Lexi shook her head, about to protest.

"Maybe she has some old Nazi stuff. Stuff she'd give us, like armbands or a flag or something."

"I didn't see anything—"

Mick cut her off. "Where does she live?"

"Over on Parker, but—"

Serge stood up and started stomping out the fire, chugging the rest of his beer. "Come on, let's go."

Biting her lip, Lexi had no choice but to follow. Why had she even told them about the old lady? Maybe she should just go home. But she knew she couldn't. That would give Serge more reason to get rid of her.

They left the woods and hurried down West Road to Parker, keeping to the moonless shadows. Lexi pointed to the house. The porch was dark, but the lamp inside glowed through the filmy curtains in the front windows. She imagined the old lady sitting in her chair, reading, or dozing like her grandmother used to do.

"Forget it, you guys," she whispered. "She's probably asleep. We can come back some other time. Let's go."

Serge snorted. "No way. We're here now. Let's visit."

"But she's just an old lady. She's probably senile and doesn't know what she's talking about."

"She won't mind us visiting," Serge said, his beady eyes narrowing. "She's a Nazi and we're Nazis. We're like family."

For a moment they paused on the sidewalk. Lexi hoped they would change their minds, but Serge took the first step down the walkway to the porch. Everyone followed. She trailed behind.

Serge suddenly pulled her up front. "I've got a plan."

CHAPTER FOUR

URSULA SANK BACK IN the chair and rested her head against one of the wings. She pulled an afghan up over her knees to ward off the chill—a chill that had nothing to do with the falling temperatures outside and everything to do with . . .

Trying to forget, she forced her eyes wide open, but her eyelids were heavy, and they drooped. She fought sleep, afraid of what she would find on the other side of darkness. Afraid of her memories that she had kept so well buried for all these years until one girl with a tattoo on her bald head had brought her past to life.

The tattoo. A spider, the girl had called it. And so it was, a wicked, poisonous spider that spun a web of steel lies that snared and wouldn't let go.

Ursula's head ached, and she couldn't keep her eyes open any longer.

Cold air pinched her cheeks as she walked to school with Hildegard. They both kept their heads bent against the sharp wind.

Suddenly Wolfgang and three of his friends raced up from behind them. They held their hands in the air like bombers, dropping exploding, hair-mussing bombs on the girls' heads as they ran by.

"Stop it!" Hildegard screamed after her brother, patting down her straight, brown hair that had been tousled by five wiggling fingers. "I'll tell Mother on you!"

Wolfgang just turned around and laughed. His friends laughed, too, then disappeared around the corner.

"I really hate him," Hildegard muttered.

"But he's your brother," Ursula protested.

"I still hate him. And even if I do tell Mother on him, she won't believe me, or she'll tell me to stop complaining. Everything Wolfgang does is right, because he's a boy."

"I wish I had a brother," Ursula said.

Hildegard looked at her as if she were crazy. "Believe me, you don't!"

Ursula didn't argue. Hildegard would never change her mind about how awful her twin brother was. But Ursula thought he was handsome, and he was friendly to her sometimes.

"I'm going to show them," Hildegard said, interrupting Ursula's thoughts.

"Show who?"

"My parents. I'm going to show them that Wolfgang isn't the only one who can do wonderful things. Then maybe they'll love me as much as they love him."

"What are you going to do?" Ursula picked up her pace. They'd be late to school if they didn't hurry.

"I don't know yet, but I'll think of something."

Ahead of them, Herr Boeddeker stood at the curb, talking to two officers in Gestapo uniforms.

"Guten Morgen," Herr Boeddeker said as the girls passed.

"And to you, too," Ursula said politely. She didn't really like him, but her parents had taught her to be polite to everyone, even those with beady eyes and pointy little chins.

As they walked on toward school, Hildegard giggled. "He looks like a rat," she whispered.

Ursula shivered. "He thinks he's so important now that he's the block warden, always nosing into everyone's business."

"That's his job," Hildegard said. "But you're right, he is annoying. Mama hates it when he stops by. She says he really likes to get free food. She feeds him quickly so that he'll leave."

They reached a busy corner and waited while a line of cars crossed the intersection. Then they had to wait for a tired-looking horse pulling a milk wagon to clip-clop by.

"At least he's a good German," Hildegard continued.

Ursula nodded. "That's true. He proved it when he turned in his cousin to the Gestapo. Imagine your own cousin passing out pamphlets against Hitler! I would be so ashamed."

Hildegard took Ursula's arm in the crook of her own. "And we're good Germans, too. I'd turn in my cousin if she were speaking against our Führer."

"Me, too," Ursula said. She thought about her little cousin with his big, blue eyes and his stubby little nose. He was only three. She didn't have to worry about turning him in, so it was easy to agree.

"I'd even turn in my brother," Hildegard said with a laugh. "If it meant he'd be out of the house."

"You don't mean that," Ursula said.

"Yes, I do."

Ursula shook her friend's arm and laughed. "He'll never turn traitor to Germany, so he'll be with you until he goes into the army."

"Poor me," Hildegard moaned. Then they both giggled as they walked across the street.

They continued in silence for a moment, then Hildegard said, "I watched last night until I fell asleep."

Ursula glanced at her. "Watched what?"

Hildegard jerked her thumb over her shoulder. "You know, the Reineke's house."

For a moment, Ursula had no idea what her best friend was talking about. Then she remembered the flickering light in the window. "Did you see anything?"

Hildegard shook her head. "No. Nothing unusual, anyway."

Ursula let go of Hildegard's arm and shifted her schoolbooks. "I probably just imagined the light. It may have been a reflection from another window."

Hildegard shrugged. "Perhaps. Or maybe it really did come from their house, but what could it mean?"

Ursula stopped walking and whispered, "They're making secret pamphlets like Herr Boeddeker's cousin?"

Hildegard lowered her voice, too. "Or they're having secret meetings."

Ursula clutched her friend's arm. "What if they're hiding someone?"

Hildegard stared at her with wide eyes. "You mean . . . Jews?"

"Why else would they use a candle instead of the regular light? They were hoping no one would see it."

Hildegard thought a moment and then shook her head. "No, the Reinekes are good Germans. My papa says so. And Frau Reineke belongs to the Women's Organization."

"Maybe that's just so people will think they're good Germans," Ursula said. "Remember, Fräulein Klute said anyone can be the enemy."

Fräulein Klute was their Jungmädel leader. She was tall and beautiful. Ursula hoped she'd look like her when she got older.

"Even friends and neighbors," Hildegard said.

"Even family," Ursula added. "I think we should watch the Reinekes more closely. If they are hiding Jews and we don't report them, then we're not being good Germans."

"I know. Let's watch them tonight."

"Together. I'll ask Mother if you can stay over," Ursula said. "My bedroom faces their house."

"We'll wait up all night."

"We'll be heroes if they're hiding Jews and we turn them in," Ursula said softly.

"Yes," Hildegard agreed, looking thoughtful. "Heroes."

"I think I see something," Ursula whispered, peering through the window later that evening. She squinted to see better.

Hildegard crowded next to her. They both stared out into the black night. The Reineke's house squatted across the street, silent and dark. Or was it?

"See? There." Ursula pointed to the small window right up under the eaves. "See the shadow?"

Hildegard gasped. "Someone's moving behind the curtain."

"With a candle."

The girls watched in silence. The light behind the window was so dim, it looked like a reflection of moonlight, only there wasn't a moon out that night. Storm clouds had swooped in earlier like a giant, black cape just as the sun was setting.

The faint light in the window blinked out. Neither of the girls said anything for a moment.

"Do you think they're hiding something?" Hildegard whispered as though she were afraid the Reinekes might hear her.

"Or someone."

"Should we report them?"

"We have to, if we want to be good Germans. We must, for our Fatherland," Ursula said solemnly, still staring at the window across the street.

"For our Führer," Hildegard agreed. She rummaged through her bag for her little book. "I'll write down exactly what we saw. We can tell Fräulein Klute and the other leaders at our next meeting, unless you think we should tell Herr Boeddeker right away?"

Ursula shook her head. "We'll tell our troop leaders. I don't like the block warden, even if he is a loyal German."

The storm blew closer. Ursula watched the lightning streak across the sky like a knife, slicing, slashing. The hair on her arms prickled. Thunder echoed like a hundred milk carts rumbling down the road. Rain pelted the ground below, swelling puddles into a miniature, raging river, sweeping leaves and the odd piece of debris along in its current.

The thunder grumbled louder as the storm settled right over them. Hildegard dropped her notebook and placed her hands over her ears as a flash of lightning was immediately followed by a mighty clap that shook the house.

Ursula watched a brilliant streak of lightning directly behind the Reineke's house. For a moment it seemed to hang in the air—or maybe the flash was just burned into *her eyes—one long stroke from the sky to the ground, with a slight jag across it, like a cross.*

She pulled away from the window as thunder pounded above her again and again and again. . . .

CHAPTER FIVE

HOLDING OPEN THE SCREEN DOOR, Lexi pounded on the old woman's door when the doorbell didn't get an answer. She could see a faint outline of the old woman through the sheer curtain in the door's window. She was slumped in the chair under the soft glow of the lamp, asleep.

"Is the old Kraut dead?" Serge rasped. He and the others crouched under the window so they wouldn't be seen. "Knock again."

Lexi rapped until her knuckles hurt, wishing the old woman would wake up and answer the door, but at the same time praying she wouldn't. If she didn't answer, they would all go home.

Finally, the woman roused with a start, like someone waking from a bad dream. She looked around as though she didn't know where she was, then focused on the door where Lexi stood, still knocking.

Lexi waved, wondering if the old woman could see her. She pushed herself up from the chair and slowly

hobbled to the door. Lexi remembered her grandmother walking the same way, the pain of arthritis cramping her joints, although she never complained about it.

The woman—what was her name? Something old-fashioned and weird—finally made it to the door. She tugged aside the curtain and peered out at Lexi, narrowing her eyes when she saw who it was. Her gaze swept the empty porch before she reached for the dead bolt and turned it. She pulled the door open.

Lexi opened her mouth to say something, but Serge jumped up before a word could slip between her lips.

He pushed forward, nearly knocking the old woman aside. *"Heil Hitler!"* he said as he stormed into the house, followed by Mick, Karen, Billy, and Devon. Lexi hung back, the heat of embarrassment rising up her neck.

"I . . ." she began haltingly. "These are my friends. They wanted to meet you." The words sounded so lame, especially since her friends were prowling through the house, nosing into closets and drawers and examining the photos on the walls.

"Ach, Amy," the woman said sadly under her breath, shaking her head.

Karen jerked her gaze to them, her nose ring winking in the light. "Amy? Who's Amy?"

Lexi saw that everyone had heard and was poised in mid-action, staring at her. "My name . . ." She turned to the woman. "My name is really Alexandra. Amy is my middle name, but no one calls me that. My grand-mother did," she rushed on. "Only . . . but she . . ."

The old woman slowly closed the door. When she looked up, Lexi saw that her eyes were cloudy with age and the left one seemed to be tearing, a constant stream running along the fine creases in the weathered face.

"Ursula Zeidler," Mick said, reading from an envelope on a shelf near the chair. "A very good German name." He turned to look at Ursula. "Lexi—*I mean Amy*—," he looked at her and grinned "tells us you were one of Hitler's children." He thumped himself on the chest. "We, too, are Hitler's children. Make that his *grandchildren,*" he said with a laugh.

"Do you have any good Nazi stuff?" Serge broke in. He picked up a ceramic elephant, then plunked it carelessly back onto the shelf. "Not this garbage. Any pins or flags or guns?"

Ursula stood up a little straighter. "No, I don't have anything you want. I think you should go now."

Lexi saw the slight wobble of Ursula's lower lip and her heart seemed to twist in her chest. If only this old woman didn't remind her so much of Nanna.

"Come on, guys," she said. "Let's go. She doesn't have anything."

"Then tell us some stories," Billy said. He was crouched in front of a stack of drawers, pulling out folders and old envelopes, throwing them aside when they didn't look interesting. The wooden floor around him looked like the aftermath of a *blitzkrieg*. "Tell us stories of how it was when Hitler ruled. The Aryans should have won the war!"

"Hitler was evil." Ursula spat each word out like bullets from a howitzer.

Serge jerked around, anger tightening his lips. "You can still die for saying that."

Ursula flinched, but she didn't back up. She lifted her chin a little higher.

Karen pointed to one of the photos on the wall and sneered at Ursula. "You're in uniform here, so you can't deny you were a Nazi. If you hate Hitler so much, why did you join this group?"

Ursula opened and closed her mouth several times without saying anything. "I was a fool," she finally said, her voice low and hoarse. "I didn't know any better. But now I know."

"Now you know what?" Billy asked.

"I know what he did. He tortured and killed millions of innocent people. Children like you, too."

Serge laughed. "Are you talking about the Holocaust myth? That's a bunch of crap."

Ursula didn't even turn in his direction. Instead, she stood stiff and straight, staring at some invisible midpoint between Lexi and the wall. Her lips pressed together in a thin, white line. Occasionally she swayed a bit side to side, and Lexi feared she would topple over. She almost put out a hand to steady the older woman, but held back at the last minute when she noticed Serge's beady eyes drilling into her.

"Now she's not talking," Karen mocked. "Ooo, I'm soooo sad."

Lexi clenched her teeth. *This is your family,* she reminded herself. *They took you in when everything else was falling apart.* But she couldn't help the flick of irritation that snagged at the back of her neck.

As if he could read her thoughts, Mick sidled up to her and said, "She's *your* friend, Lexi, maybe you can get her to talk."

Lexi shook her head and looked down at the blunt, black toes of her Doc Martens. "She's not my friend. I just met her tonight."

Serge grinned, which made his eyes squeeze to even smaller slits. "I bet I can think of a way to make her talk."

"I have nothing to say to you," Ursula said.

Serge laughed, but it wasn't a pleasant sound. "Some people think they're better than others. Like the kikes and the gooks and the niggers and all the rest of them. You can kill 'em, but you can't wipe 'em out. They just keep multiplying and coming back."

Lexi bit her lip. She hated it when Serge started talking about killing. Spraypainting synagogues or Baptist churches or knocking over headstones at cemeteries was one thing. At least no one was getting hurt. And it was better than sitting home, listening to her mother's drunken laughter or ranting, depending on her mood. But it made Lexi nervous when Serge started talking about killing. She couldn't tell if he was all talk or if he'd really act on his words.

Lexi glanced at her watch. Already after eleven. Her mother'd have a fit, if she was sober enough to notice. "Come on, let's go."

"Not until we get a story," Serge insisted, moving toward Ursula. "I want a good story about how the Aryans kicked butt."

Mick approached Ursula from the other side. Soon the others had formed a circle around the old woman.

Serge tapped her on the shoulder. "Tell us a story."

"Forget it," Lexi said. "Let's leave her alone."

No one listened to her. Billy nudged Ursula this time. "Story time."

Soon they were moving around the ring, taking turns tapping and lightly shoving the old woman in the center of the circle. Ursula's left eye was still wet, and Lexi wondered if real tears were falling, or if this was just a leaky duct that didn't work properly anymore. Nanna had had one of those. She had carried tissues in her cuff to dab at the tears. Lexi couldn't help noticing the wad of tissues delicately peeking out of Ursula's cuff.

"Come on! Let's go," she pleaded.

"I said I want a story first." This time Serge really shoved the old woman.

Ursula stumbled forward a few steps on stiff legs.

Lexi held her breath. As Serge prepared to shove again, Lexi lunged. She couldn't help herself. "No!" she cried. "Leave her alone!"

Serge's shove missed its target, knocking into Lexi instead. Lexi tried to regain her balance, her arms flailing. A bony hand gripped her elbow, trying to steady her, but it was too late. She crashed to the floor, knocking Ursula aside by accident.

An eerie wail of pain filled the room.

Serge stared down at Lexi before she could get up. With his face twisted in fury, he looked like he wanted to stomp on her. "Don't ever interfere again!" he stormed at her. "Or next time you'll be the one bawling."

"Out of here," Mick directed quickly.

Lexi scrambled to her feet, her heart pounding. She looked down at the injured woman who held both hands to her hip, her eyes blinking against the pain.

"I . . . I'm sorry," Lexi blurted out. With that, she followed her friends outside where they dispersed into the night, like leaves tossed by an unruly wind.

CHAPTER SIX

URSULA WATCHED THEM GO. Cold air gusted through the open door, but waves of pain and nausea kept her from getting up to close it. She couldn't even drag herself over to the phone to call for help.

Those *children*. Those *monsters*. Didn't they realize what they were doing? Didn't they care?

But of course they cared. And she had cared once, too. She had wanted a strong Fatherland—a strong Germany. And in order to be strong and rule the world for a thousand years, they had to get rid of the enemies.

So many enemies.

So much killing.

She shuddered. And now a new generation was rising up to carry on the fight for a master race. And how passionate they were about it. *And how totally and utterly wrong.* But who was she to tell them the truth? Not that they listened.

The girl, Amy . . . Lexi. Maybe she had realized. She was still young. Maybe it wasn't too late for her.

Ursula's cat, Princess Charming, strolled in, padding lightly over to her fallen mistress. She nudged her face against Ursula's and licked her with her sandpaper tongue, before nestling against the woman's stomach and tucking her nose under her tail.

Laying her head on her arm, Ursula tried to curl into a comfortable position, but the pain in her side gripped her muscles. Her breath caught until she could relax enough to breathe again.

Ursula knew her hip was broken, despite the many glasses of milk and pounds of cheese she had consumed, and all the calcium pills she'd taken these last years.

Could a person die from a broken hip? Maybe not, but the cold air blowing in through the open door might give her pneumonia. Not a good thing for someone her age.

Another wave of pain coursed through her like the flow of the tide, coming in strong, then going out, but never far away.

The cold and the pain reminded her of something. What was it?

Cold and pain. Pain and cold. Always cold. Always pain, but not in her hip, in her stomach. She was hungry.

Her living room faded before her eyes, and a new image filled her vision.

She found herself in a drab room. A cold stove squatted in one corner. Next to it a wooden table stood with its top bare except for a plain white bowl. Cupboards covered the far wall, but Ursula knew they were empty. She shivered as the late afternoon sun filtered through the curtained windows. She remembered this room. She was a little girl, only five, and the year was 1932.

Her mother's voice crooned in her ear, and thick arms hugged her on a wide lap. "Ach, mein Liebling," her mother said softly. "Ich liebe dich. Ich liebe dich."

Ursula snuggled against her mother's ample breast, but the cold was biting, tearing its way through her wool sweater and scratching its cold fingers against her skin. And the pangs of hunger in her tummy chewed at her insides like hungry dogs gnawing on a bare bone.

"Where is Papa?" she asked, more to distract herself from the cold and hunger than because she really wanted to know. At any rate, she already knew the answer.

Her mother stroked her hair, the same honey color as her own. "He's out looking for work, Liebling."

Ursula didn't say anything. Every day he was out looking for work. One day there would be a miracle, he promised her, and he would find a job.

In the meantime, there wasn't enough coal for heat, nor enough food to eat.

And when Papa did come home after a long day of looking for work, he sat in the corner alone or with a few friends and drank beer, swearing about something called the Treaty of Versailles.

Ursula didn't know what the treaty was, but she

wished it had never happened, for it made her father very angry. He got angrier each day. He never tickled her anymore. He never brushed her hair or told her stories in his deep, quiet voice. He hardly ever hugged her.

Ursula sighed, and her mother chuckled. "Such a big sigh from such a little girl."

Ursula couldn't help smiling. When she was in her mother's arms, she could almost believe everything would be fine, and a miracle would happen just as Papa promised.

Her mother shifted and lifted her off her lap. "We must start a fire if I'm to cook," she said.

Ursula didn't have to ask what they would have for supper. Thin potato soup and dry, coarse bread. At least the soup would warm her up before she had to climb the cold stairs to her bedroom.

While her mother stoked the embers lying dormant under the ashes and added more precious coal, Ursula arranged the three large, lumpy potatoes on the counter, making two eyes and a nose. How she longed for a carrot to shape into a mouth, or a row of mushrooms, or better yet, some pieces of meat from the butcher. Her stomach growled fiercely.

Her mother bustled over to her and chopped the potatoes into small pieces, leaving the skins on. Mama didn't waste anything.

As the soup came to a boil and the windows fogged up from the steam, the front door banged open. Bootsteps echoed in the hall.

"Where are my Lieblings?*" Papa roared.*

Surprised by such an exuberant greeting, Ursula hopped down from her chair and raced into Papa's outstretched arms. He rubbed his cold, prickly cheeks against hers, making her giggle. Herr Schmitt and Herr Jolmes had come home with him, so she knew this would be a night where Papa sat in the corner closest the stove and muttered and railed against the Treaty of Versailles. And yet, tonight was different. Papa's smile lit up his face and made wrinkles around his eyes instead of the usual ones between his eyebrows. And his friends were laughing and patting each other on the back instead of scowling in silence.

"What's this?" Mama asked, greeting them at the kitchen door, wiping her hands on her apron. "Ach, so much noise!" she scolded with a smile.

Papa plunked Ursula on the kitchen table and took his wife in his arms. He still had his coat on. He twirled her around and around until she was breathless with laughter.

For a long moment, Ursula forgot about her hunger pains as she watched her parents dance.

"Stop, Helmut," Mama protested, blushing and trying to push out of Papa's strong arms.

The men standing around in the small kitchen laughed and winked at each other. Suddenly the room seemed warmer, cozier, brighter.

"What is it? What is it?" Mama asked, finally free of Papa's arms.

Papa laughed, and his friends joined him. "Let's eat."

"Eat?" Mama squeaked. "How can I eat until you tell me what makes you so happy?"

Papa drew Mama into his arms once again. "You make me happy," he said in a husky voice.

Ursula watched, shocked. It wasn't proper for Papa to say such things to Mama in front of his friends. But Papa just laughed and Mama fanned her hands in front of her red face, keeping her gaze lowered to the floor.

She quickly served five bowls of steaming soup and placed chunks of bread on the table.

Only after he'd been served his second bowl did Papa begin to explain. "It's a miracle," he said as he broke off a piece of the hard bread.

"You found work?" Mama said in a hushed voice as if she were afraid to even say the magical words.

Papa leaned forward. "Even better. We heard a man speak today. He promises to rebuild Germany. There will be jobs for everyone. We will be a strong nation once again. The Treaty of Versailles—," he spat on the floor and Mama didn't even protest, "is nothing to us. We will be strong!"

Ursula's heart thumped with excitement. All she knew was that the treaty had made her father angry, but now it was gone. Papa smiled and laughed. It really was a miracle.

"He has many plans for us," Papa went on, slurping up his soup.

"Like what?" Mama asked, still acting as if she were too afraid to believe the good news.

Papa waved his spoon around. "Oh many, many plans. He's promised us all jobs, and with it our pride."

One of his friends nodded. "We will rout the enemies so that Germany can be the power it once was."

"Ja," Papa agreed.

Mama looked around the table. "Enemies?"

Papa nodded. "People who are destroying our country, pulling it apart. Jews, for one."

"Jews? Like the Gutemanns?"

Ursula held her breath. What was an enemy? And why were they talking about the Gutemanns? Helen Gutemann was her friend. And Frau Gutemann was pretty with her curly brown hair.

Papa shook his head. "Oh, no, not like the Gutemanns. They are good Germans like we are. But there are other Jews who . . . who . . ."

Ursula stared in surprise. She had never seen her father at a loss for words.

"Who are evil," Herr Schmitt finished for him.

Papa nodded.

As the conversation continued, Ursula played with her spoon, staring at her upside down face in the shiny surface. She was glad Helen wasn't her enemy, whatever that was. And that she wasn't evil. Ursula knew that evil was something bad, and Helen was never bad.

Ursula closed her eyes and rested her head on the cool tabletop. Mama had cleared away the dishes long *ago, but everyone seemed too excited and happy to re-member to put her to bed.*

A miracle had finally happened, just as Papa had said it would. Papa would have work and they would have plenty of coal and food. No more cold. No more wrenching hunger pains.

Just as she drifted away to sleep, she heard her father softly say, "He is a great man. A very great man this Adolf Hitler."

CHAPTER SEVEN

Outside Ursula's house, Devon grabbed Lexi's hand and they ran down the block, losing sight of the others as they jumped hedges and cut through yards, winding through the maze of suburban streets. Finally, Devon and Lexi slowed down.

"Don't worry," Devon said, gasping for air. "I won't let Serge touch you. Besides, we're family. We don't hurt each other."

Lexi smiled weakly. It wasn't that she didn't believe her friend, but Serge was six feet tall and broad and all muscle. No one would stop him if he wanted to do something, except maybe Mick. "Thanks," she said anyway.

"He's just talk," Devon said as they continued on, walking now.

"Maybe," Lexi agreed, but she wondered.

They reached a crossroad. Devon tapped her on the chin. "See you tomorrow, and stop worrying."

"But what about that lady? What if she dies?"

Devon laughed. "Are you kidding? She's probably in bed by now. She's fine." He reached out and hugged her awkwardly.

For a moment Lexi was in shock. She couldn't remember the last time someone had hugged her, but she was sure it hadn't been since Nanna had died. No one in her family hugged now.

He released her and saluted. *"Heil Hitler!"*

She returned the salute.

They turned and walked away from each other as if they were gunfighters and would turn around at ten paces and shoot each other. But they didn't.

It took Lexi fifteen minutes to march home. She kept to the shadows, any moment expecting to hear the wail of sirens as paramedics and police

answered Ursula's 911 call. But the night was strangely still.

As she approached her house, automatic lights flooded the driveway and lawn, bathing her in a glaring light. She glanced at the gold Mercedes as she hurried up the driveway. She didn't recognize the car, but that didn't surprise her. Her mother's boyfriends always drove expensive cars. But the boyfriends didn't last long. Entering through the side door she tiptoed into the laundry room.

Giddy laughter floated through the air, coming from the large, formal living room. A deeper, gruff laugh joined in.

Her stomach clenched. She pulled her hood tighter around her face. If she planned this right, she could slip up the stairs without getting caught.

As though walking on glass, she moved carefully through the kitchen into the two-story front foyer. The tough part was edging around the bottom curl of the banister and slipping up the first couple of steps without being seen.

Another gurgle of laughter came from the living room. Lexi scooted forward, slinking against the handrail to avoid being detected.

"Lexi? Is that you?"

Lexi froze.

"Lexi, come here! Come meet my business associate."

With a defeated sigh, Lexi released the banister and slunk into the white-and-gold living room. Tall windows graced either side of the enormous marble fireplace. Sconces jutted out from the walls and portraits of people who weren't even related to them stared imperiously down.

"Where have you been?" her mother demanded, forgetting to make introductions.

"Just out," Lexi said. She eyed the man sitting on the plush couch next to her mother. His suit coat was off and he had one arm draped over the back. His balding head shone in the subtle lighting. On the coffee table before them stood two discarded bottles of champagne. A third one was open and half-empty.

Lexi flinched as her mother stood up, but she held her ground and stared defiantly at her.

Her mother's black pantsuit hugged slim hips and a narrow waist. She tapped a nail on her diamond-studded watch. "You were supposed to be home by nine. You have school tomorrow." She swayed on her feet.

Lexi watched as the bald man shot out an arm to hold her mother steady. His hand landed on her butt, and they both burst out giggling. Lexi turned to leave.

"I'm not through with you, young lady," her mother stated between giggles. "What do you have to say for yourself?"

"Don't worry, I'll get up in time for school. I always do."

"That's not the point," her mother argued, stepping forward, leaving her giggles behind.

Lexi refused to show her fear by stepping back.

"You are over two hours late." She sniffed with disdain. "You were probably out with those . . . those disgusting animals with the bald heads."

Lexi gritted her teeth. "They are not disgusting animals. They're my friends. And they like me more than you do!"

Her mother's hand shot out and connected with Lexi's cheek. "How dare you say that!"

Lexi refused to lift a hand to soothe her stinging cheek. "It's true. I know it. You just don't want me to have any fun." She hated that she felt like crying. She hated knowing that she just wanted her mother to wrap her up in her arms and tell her everything was going to be all right, even as the burn of the slap stung her cheek. She hated the ache of love she still felt for her mother, even though she'd been trying to cut it away ever since her father had left them. The divorce was all her mother's fault. All the drinking . . . all the boyfriends.

If only Daddy were still with them. If only Nanna were still alive. She tried to picture the way life had been a long time ago, but all she could see was Ursula Zeidler, her face contorted in pain and fear. Was Mrs. Zeidler someone's Nanna?

". . . just a child. Do you hear me?" her mother finished, her high-pitched voice scraping on Lexi's nerves like nails on a chalkboard.

No, Lexi hadn't heard her, and she didn't care. She whirled around and dashed up the stairs to her room.

She slammed the door and flopped onto her bed.

Tears burned the back of her eyes, but she refused to let them fall. Tears were for babies. And no matter what her mother thought or said, she wasn't a little kid anymore. She was thirteen, old enough to be making her own decisions.

A light tapping on the door adjoining her room with Shelby's brought Lexi's head up. "Come in," she called.

Shelby shuffled in with bunny slippers covering her feet and her long nightgown trailing on the floor behind her. Her eyes looked bleary with sleep. She sat on the bed next to Lexi.

"Where were you?" she asked.

Lexi rolled onto her side. "Out with Mick and them."

Shelby tugged on Lexi's sweatshirt. "Can I touch your head?"

Lexi smiled and released her hood. Her sister ran a warm hand over the bare skin, giggling softly behind her other hand. "That feels so cool. I want to shave my head, too."

"Forget it," Lexi said shortly. "You're barely ten. You're too young."

Shelby pouted. "I can shave my head if I want to. You did."

"I'm older, and I know what I'm doing. Maybe when you're older you can."

"When can I go to a meeting with you? You said I could. You told me they wanted me to come. They don't think I'm too young."

Lexi laughed and held up her hands to stop the flow of words. "You can," she said. "Some day."

Shelby clapped her hands together. "I can't wait. I promise I'll be good and do everything you say."

Impulsively, Lexi hugged her sister.

Shelby squirmed. "What are you doing?"

"Hugging you."

"I know, but why?"

"I love you."

Shelby disentangled herself from her sister's arms and looked at her with lifted eyebrows. "I love you, too." She shuffled to the door, trying to keep the slippers on her feet. At the door, she turned and raised her right arm to a forty-five degree angle as Lexi had taught her. *"Sieg Heil!"* Then she dropped her hand and frowned. "What does that mean again?"

"Hail to victory," Lexi repeated by rote. Mick had tried to teach her a lot of German phrases, but she only remembered a couple of them.

"What victory?"

Lexi shrugged. "Victory over . . ." she tried to remember what Mick had told her. "Oh, I don't know. Victory over anyone who's not white."

Shelby nodded as though her older sister had said something infinitely wise.

Lexi hid a smile. She could tell Shelby had no idea what she was talking about, just as *she* sometimes had no idea what Mick and Serge and the others were talking about. But she had nodded, too. She didn't want

them to think she was stupid or not interested. They might not let her hang with them if they thought that. And hanging with them was all she had.

After her sister was gone, Lexi looked at her watch, then at her phone on the other side of her bed. Thirty minutes had passed since she'd run out of Ursula's house. Was she at the hospital yet? Would she tell people what had happened? Ursula knew her name—Alexandra Amy—but not her last name. The police couldn't find her, could they?

Another thought gave her a painful pinch. What if Ursula couldn't reach the phone? What if she were still lying on the floor? No matter what Devon said, she worried.

She chewed on her lower lip and ran a hand absently across her smooth scalp. If she called 911, could they trace the call back to her? She remembered that on television shows it always seemed that people had to stay on the line for a certain amount of time before a call could be traced. And what about Caller ID? But what about Ursula, who reminded her of Nanna?

Lexi picked up the handset and tapped the 9. Then a 1. She hesitated over the last number. Before she could change her mind, she jabbed at the 1 again.

The call was picked up on the second ring. "911," said a voice. "Is this an emergency?"

"Uh, yes. An old lady fell on Parker Street. I think she hurt herself. She needs help."

65

"Outside? On the sidewalk?"

"No, in her house. I think the house number is 375."

"And who is this?"

Lexi slammed the handset down. She unplugged her phone from the wall. This was her private line, and the number wasn't listed, so maybe there was no way to trace the call. She hoped so.

She unlaced her heavy boots and kicked them off. Quickly she changed into a T-shirt, dropping her clothes in a heap on the floor. She wiggled her toes, finally free of the weight. Mick said that to hang out with them, she had to wear her jeans rolled up at the ankle and the Doc Martens. She didn't mind, really, but sometimes she missed wearing some of the pretty sweaters in her closet. But pink and purple weren't good Nazi colors, she'd been told. She was also supposed to wear a bomber jacket, but her mother refused to buy one for her.

She moved to her desk and noticed that her computer was already on. Sometimes Shelby used it for her homework. She dug to the back of her top drawer, extracting a disk she kept hidden. Pushing it into the slot on her computer tower, she opened up a file and tabbed down to the end of the document. She started typing.

Tuesday, 11:42 P.M.

Tonight we sprayed Temple Beth El. I wrote KIKE in big letters across the front doors. I wonder what kike means. I mean, I know it's an insult, like nigger, but I wonder where it came from. And where did nigger

come from? Or gook? Or spick? I asked Mick about it,
but he said it didn't matter as long as people hated it.

I also sprayed huge swastikas on the walls. Serge told
me ahead of time to do that. Said it would scare the
Jews. Maybe even scare them away for good.

The whole time I was so jumpy. I thought the police
would come bust us for sure. Then, when I was running
away, I almost got caught, but I hid on this old lady's
porch. She let me in.

She kind of reminds me of Nanna. I miss Nanna.

And then later we went back to the lady's house—
all my stupid fault. I hope she's okay.

We have something really big planned for Thursday
night. Mick said not to tell anyone. As if I would. We're
going to meet at the Big Tree at ten. I'll have to sneak
out. If I don't show, they'll kick me out of the Pack for
sure. I think Serge is trying to get rid of me anyway.

I wonder where Daddy is. Mom said he went to
Switzerland for some conference. He doesn't even call.
But hey, that's the way it goes, right? At least I have
Mick and them to hang out with. Devon said they're my
family now.

CHAPTER EIGHT

THE WIND WHIPPED DOWN Parker Street. Fall leaves swirled like minitornadoes, and the sky threatened rain. Lexi kept her head down to avoid getting blasted in the face with cold air. When she walked by Ursula's house, she couldn't help looking at the windows. Was the old lady home? Or had she been taken to the hospital?

Lexi hurried on. If Ursula had reported what they'd done, maybe the police would be on the lookout for them. She walked quickly past the water tower and into the woods to the Big Tree.

"You guys are a bunch of wimps," Serge was saying, spitting into the circle where they usually had a fire.

Mick glanced around at the rest of the group. Lexi thought he looked uneasy.

"What's going on?" she asked.

"Serge has an idea," Devon said.

"But these hicks are too chicken to do it," Serge said. "Man, you should see what we used to do. This is nothing. Are you skins or not?" He took a swig of beer.

"Fine, we'll do it," Mick said. He guzzled the rest of his beer and tossed the can into a large pile that had grown like a giant fungus at the base of the tree.

Serge took off like he was the leader, and everyone followed him.

"What's going on?" Lexi asked Devon as they hurried along.

Devon grinned. "Serge says he saw where this blind kid lives. We're going to scare him."

Lexi slowed down. "Blind? But why do we want to scare him? Is he black? Jewish? What?"

Devon shook his head. "Come on, Lex, you know anyone who isn't good Aryan blood is no good."

"This kid isn't Aryan?"

Devon grabbed her arm. "He's blind. Do you want cripples and the blind and other impure people mixing in with strong Aryan blood? I don't think so."

"Oh." Lexi had never thought about any of this before. "But maybe he wasn't born blind. Maybe he got it from an accident or something."

"Maybe, but he's blind now, so what good is he?"

They left the woods near the Boulevard. The threatening weather had kept most walkers inside, so they owned the streets except for the cars that didn't even slow down when they passed. This was the poorest section of town. Serge led them down side streets to a narrow alley between a couple of row houses.

"This is it," he said, motioning to the old wooden

building on the left. "Let's do it." He picked up an empty bottle and tossed it at the side window.

The sound of shattering glass rang in Lexi's ears. She looked around nervously, but they were the only ones in the alley.

Mick and Billy took cans of spray paint out from under their bomber jackets and started scrawling messages on the side of the house.

"This is crazy," Lexi said. Wind pushed at her as if trying to blow her out of the alley. "Anyone could walk by. Why didn't we wait till dark?"

Serge heard her. "Chicken? And besides, it's dark enough with the storm coming. Let's go to the front door."

Lexi held back until Serge looked at her with his beady eyes. "Coming?" he rasped.

She went.

They stole around to the front of the house, checking to make sure no one was around. They stepped up to the porch. Tall windows framed the weathered door. Serge shoved his boot through one of the windows. He motioned to Lexi to do the same to the other window.

She hesitated only a second, lifting her boot to kick. Suddenly the door flew open.

"Hey, what are you doing?" a boy asked, his head tilted up like he was a dog sniffing the air.

"I . . . I nothing," she blurted out. Jeez, he was just a little kid. Maybe eight or nine. She could see right away that he was blind. His eyes were vacant and both hands were outstretched before him. She turned to leave.

Serge grabbed her arm and pulled her with him into the house, shoving the boy backward. "Thanks for inviting us in."

The interior was dark and shabby.

"Where are your parents?" Serge asked.

The boy trembled so fiercely, his words came out in a jumble. "They . . . they'll be right home."

Lexi tried to pull away, but Serge still gripped her with strong fingers.

Serge reached out his other hand and pushed the boy again. This time the boy collapsed on the worn carpet and started to cry. Serge kicked him. "Shut up."

Lexi wrenched her arm free. "Stop it! Leave him alone," she cried.

"He's a disgusting animal," Serge said as he glared at her. "Now kick him—hard."

Lexi shook her head, backing up toward the door.

Serge lunged for her, nearly knocking her to the floor. "What kind of a Nazi are you?" he demanded. "Don't you want to be part of this powerful nation?"

Lexi nodded.

"Then prove it." He shoved her forward.

She stumbled forward a few steps until she stood over the boy.

"Kick him," Serge ordered, right behind her.

The kid covered his head with his arms, his legs

drawn up like a cowering dog's.

"I . . . I can't."

"Do it! Do it or forget ever showing your face around here."

"But he's already scared. Weren't we just going to scare him?"

"You really think that's enough? Kick him so he'll never forget this."

"Cops coming!" Devon shouted from the porch.

Lexi's heart, already pumping furiously, felt like it was going to explode. They ran out of the house and flew off the porch, racing down the alley, their bootsteps echoing between the buildings.

Large raindrops began to fall. They splattered on Lexi's face, and she was glad. No one would see her tears.

Wednesday after school, Lexi looked both ways before crossing Parker at the corner of Elm. She wasn't looking for cars, but for anyone who might notice her. She pulled her hood tighter around her head. She didn't want to be noticed. Not now.

Going to school with a bald head was okay. Everyone stared and pointed. Some even laughed. But she didn't care. Just because they didn't have enough guts to make a statement for themselves. Instead, they dressed the same and talked the same and thought the same. And then, when she'd had her scalp tattooed with

the swastika, even the teachers talked behind her back. Miss Fuller, her math teacher, tried to pretend to be her friend. She told her that the swastika might insult a lot of people. But what did Lexi care? The tattoo was only a bunch of black lines in a certain pattern. "If you don't like it, don't look," she had told Miss Fuller.

But right now, away from school, she didn't want anyone to notice her or her tattoo, so she kept her head covered and her gaze on the sidewalk.

Parker Street was really the dividing line between the Heights, where Lexi lived, and the poorer section of town, the Flats. Here, the houses were small but neat. Each had a trim front lawn, a country wreath on the door, and a doorbell that glowed at night like a magic button.

When she reached Ursula Zeidler's driveway, she slowed down. She had to find out whether the old lady was okay.

Taking a deep breath, she walked up the porch stairs, trying not to clomp too heavily. She peered through the curtained window, but because it was light outside and dark in the room, all she could see were shadowy shapes. Was anyone even in there?

"Hi."

Lexi whipped around, her heart in her throat. A small girl with dark hair and dark eyes stood behind her on the porch, smiling quizzically.

"Are you going to visit Mrs. Zeidler, too?" the girl asked.

"I . . . no. I was just leaving."

"Oh, come on, don't go just because I'm here. Mrs. Zeidler will love to see you." She reached out and rang the doorbell.

"No, I really have to go." Lexi backed down the steps.

The girl lowered her voice as footsteps approached the door from the other side. "Mrs. Zeidler was in the hospital yesterday, you know. I think she could use some cheering up."

Lexi hesitated. "In the hospital? Why?"

The front door opened. A woman in a white dress, white sweater, and white clogs smiled at them with white teeth, glowing in her brown face.

"We're here to see Mrs. Zeidler," the girl said.

The nurse let her in and then stared at Lexi, still on the lower step. For a second, Lexi had the urge to call her a nigger and spit in her face like Devon told her he did. After all, wasn't this nurse an enemy to the master race with her colored skin? But a second later she felt ashamed of herself. Writing *nigger* and *kike* on walls was one thing, but saying it face to face, eye to eye . . .

She realized the nurse was still staring at her. Feeling trapped, Lexi slowly followed the other girl into the house. When she saw Ursula propped up in a hospital bed where the wing chair used to be, she felt a little faint.

"I can't believe you broke your hip," the dark-haired

girl said, hugging Ursula and handing her a box of chocolates.

"Oooo, my favorite," Ursula gushed, inspecting the box. Then she lifted her eyes and caught sight of Lexi. A flicker of fear passed through her eyes, and she smiled thinly. "Hello, Amy."

Lexi blushed. Why did she sound so scared? Did she think she had come back to hurt her? And why couldn't the old lady just call her Lexi like everyone else? Being called Amy reminded her too much of when Nanna had been alive, when her mother hadn't been drinking and her father had been home.

Lexi mumbled a greeting, finding it hard to look at the woman. "I'm sorry about your broken hip."

Ursula sighed. "Ach, it is a pain and a hindrance, and they've given me so many painkillers I feel rather dopey."

"She fell closing the curtains on Monday," the girl informed Lexi.

It took a moment for Lexi to understand these words. "Closing the curtains?"

The girl nodded. "That's right. She tripped over her cat or something, isn't that right, Mrs. Zeidler?"

Ursula nodded and patted the girl on the arm. "That's right, Ellen, dear. That's how it happened."

Lexi swallowed. But that was a lie. Ursula hadn't fallen trying to close her curtains; she had been knocked over and left alone with no one to help her. Lexi had to swallow again. Hard. And it was all *her fault.* If only she hadn't told the others about the old woman who used to be in Hitler's Youth. If only . . .

Ellen smiled at her. "I think I've seen you around."

Lexi shrugged, distracted from her thoughts. "Western Reserve High?"

Ellen shook her head. "I don't go there. But maybe I've seen you at the bowling alleys?"

"I don't bowl."

Ellen tilted her head to the side and smiled. "Then I don't know, but you do look familiar."

"Sit down and visit with me," Ursula said.

"I have to go," Lexi said quickly.

"So soon?" Ursula said, but Lexi thought she saw relief in her eyes. Or maybe it was just the glimmer of wetness in the left eye, the one that kept tearing.

"I wanted to see if you were okay," Lexi said. She turned to the girl. "Bye, uh . . ."

"Oh, how thoughtless of me," Ursula exclaimed. "I never introduced you. Amy, this is Ellen Rabinowitz, the rabbi's daughter."

Lexi stared at the girl. So this was a kike. A Jewish girl. The rabbi's daughter, no less. She waited for a ball of hate to grow in her gut like Serge said always happened to him whenever he even thought about a Jew. But all she felt was emptiness.

Had Ellen Rabinowitz cried when she saw the swastikas sprayed all over her synagogue? Would she cry Thursday night?

CHAPTER NINE

THE DRUGS MADE URSULA SLEEPY. But last night, at least, she had slept without dreams.

She watched the two girls visiting her. One, a Nazi. One, a rabbi's daughter. A Jewish girl. She remembered another Jewish girl. Helen. Helen Gutemann. Before all the hatred. Before they were enemies. Before . . .

Helen greeted her at the door. "You're just in time."

"Is this dress pretty enough?" Ursula asked, opening her coat.

"Is it your best?"

Ursula nodded, knowing her best wasn't as pretty as the dress her friend wore. But even though Papa now had a job, there still wasn't enough money to buy new clothes.

"Then it's fine," Helen said, taking her coat and drawing her into the front room. "We're about to start."

Ursula remembered Helen telling her to get there early because the Sabbath started eighteen minutes before sunset.

Nervous that she would do something wrong, she followed her friend into the dining room where the family stood, waiting. Everyone smiled at her.

Frau Gutemann wore a white shawl over her head, and Herr Gutemann wore a small round cap that Helen had told her was called a yarmulke.

Frau Gutemann lit the two candles in front of her and circled her hands three times around the flames. She prayed in a strange, melodic language that Ursula didn't understand but she liked listening to.

When the prayers to welcome in the Sabbath were concluded, Herr Gutemann placed his hands on Helen's and Ursula's heads and blessed them, then left.

"He's going to synagogue," Helen whispered. "We stay and prepare the table. When he returns, we will eat."

Ursula followed her friend to the dining table where she saw that a fine white cloth had already been spread out. She helped Helen set the places with polished silver while Frau Gutemann placed sparkling glasses and her best china on the table.

In front of Herr Gutemann's seat, she lay a wooden board and two pieces of bread, which she covered with a beautiful cloth.

"That's the chalot," Helen said. "And that's the cup for the sacramental wine," she added, pointing to the silver goblet her mother was placing next to the wooden board.

Ursula watched the preparations with wide eyes. She

had known Helen since before she could remember. They even shared a birthday and had turned ten together, just last month, but she had never known the family did this every Friday night. All she knew was that she didn't see her friend from Friday afternoon until Sunday morning.

At last Herr Gutemann came home. Ursula expected them to sit down and eat, but instead, the family started to sing a song. When they finished, Herr Gutemann went to his wife and stood before her and started singing a solo. Ursula had never heard her own father sing, much less sing to her mother. She watched in amazement.

"He's singing her Eishet Chail," Helen told her. "It's a song in Hebrew telling her how much he cares for her and thanking her for all she does to make this a home."

"He does this every Friday night?" Ursula asked.

Helen nodded with a smile. "And the song we sang before that was Shalom Aliechen to welcome the shabot angels to come and protect us."

After the song, they gathered around the dining room table once again. Herr Gutemann gave the blessing for the Sabbath, then blessed the wine and took a sip from the silver cup, which he passed to his wife. She took a sip and passed the cup to Ursula. Ursula hesitated.

"Join us," Frau Gutemann said with a smile.

Ursula took a sip of the sweet wine, then passed the cup to Helen, who also took a sip.

Next, *without talking, they all washed their hands
and gathered again at the table. Herr Gutemann
solemnly blessed the bread, cut it, dipped it in salt and
took a bite. This, like the cup of wine, was passed
around the table.*

*At last they were allowed to sit down. But instead of
eating, they started singing. Ursula wished she knew the
words so she could sing along.*

*After two songs, Herr Gutemann filled Ursula's dish
with stew.*

"It's called chulent," *Helen told her. "It's been cook-
ing since yesterday."*

Ursula took a bite, the rich flavor tickling her tongue. The stew was thick with beef, beans, and potatoes.

"Do you like it?" Helen asked.

Ursula nodded eagerly, her mouth full. Everyone laughed.

Through the rest of the meal, the Gutemanns talked about the portion of the Torah for that week, which Frau Gutemann explained was like the five books of Moses. Ursula listened, enjoying the songs they sang and the peaceful meal, even if she didn't understand what they were talking about.

Toward the end of the meal, Helen said, "The Marks are leaving. Edith told me they're moving to Amsterdam because they don't like what's going on here. They don't trust Adolf Hitler."

"It will die down," Frau Gutemann said. "Don't worry, this insanity will stop."

Herr Gutemann's thick eyebrows pulled together. He glanced at Ursula, who sat stone-still at the mention of Hitler's name. "Perhaps we should discuss this later."

Frau Gutemann clicked her tongue and placed a hand on Ursula's shoulder. "Gustav, we don't have to worry about Ursula. She's like family."

Ursula smiled. What was there to worry about, anyway? It was true that Hitler claimed Jews were the enemy of Germany, but only the bad Jews—not the kind, loving families like the Gutemanns.

After the blessing for the food, they were excused

*from the table. Ursula was surprised to find that it was
so late.*

*"Would you like me to help you wash the china?"
she asked politely.*

*Frau Gutemann smiled. "No, child, I will rinse them
myself. We won't wash them until after the Sabbath, because it is our custom not to work during this holy time.
It is a time for rest and thought."*

*Ursula grinned. "My mother would like that, I
think."*

*Helen giggled and led her to the front hall to get her
coat. Herr Gutemann would walk her home.*

*"Will you teach me a prayer in Hebrew?" Ursula
asked as she slipped on her coat.*

*"You really want to learn?" Helen asked, sounding
surprised.*

Ursula nodded. "It sounds so beautiful."

*"I'll teach you the Sabbath prayer that is said when
the candles are being lit. It goes like this." As she recited
the words, Ursula repeated them slowly, carefully enun-
ciating the Hebrew words she didn't understand.*

*"Barooch ahta Adonoi, Ellohaynoo Melech
ha-olawm . . ."*

The shimmer of laughter broke through her dream,
or was it Helen laughing? She blinked her eyes. For a
moment she didn't recognize the two girls standing by
her, but then she realized that the Sabbath dinner had
been a long-ago memory. This was now, the present,

with the pain in her hip and these two girls visiting her. Enemies.

Ursula sighed.

"I've been trying to teach Mrs. Zeidler that prayer for years," Ellen said.

Ursula realized that she must have been saying the prayer out loud.

"What does it mean?" Lexi asked.

"Blessed are You, O Lord our God, King of all the universe," Ellen recited in a hushed voice. "Who has made us holy through Your commandments, and has commanded us to kindle the lights of the Sabbath."

For a moment, no one spoke. Ursula felt an ache in her heart, far more painful than the one in her hip or in her arthritic joints. This was an old ache. One she had tried to keep buried for so many years, practically a lifetime. If anyone knew her shame . . .

"I have to go," Ellen said. She leaned over and kissed Ursula's cheek. "I'll come again tomorrow." She gave Lexi a quick wave and then left.

Ursula stared at her remaining visitor. Her hood was still up, covering her bald head and the despicable sign tattooed there. She wondered what Ellen would have said if Lexi had removed her hood.

Lexi fiddled with the ties on her sweatshirt, not looking at Ursula. "I'm sorry about Monday night," she finally said.

Ursula sighed. "It was an accident."

Lexi gazed incredulously at her. "Are you kidding? It was no accident. They wanted to hurt you."

"But you did not?"

"No! I . . . I tried to stop them."

"I know, child. I saw." She held her hand out to the girl.

Lexi slowly moved forward and took it and bent her head over it. "I am so, so sorry. I never meant for you to get hurt."

Ursula's heart warmed. There was hope here after all. She squeezed the girl's hand and said, "I want to show you something. I have some albums in that cupboard over there." She pointed.

Lexi retrieved the pile of six photo albums as Ursula directed her. She brought them back to the bed, then went to fetch a chair from the kitchen.

Once Lexi was settled, Ursula opened the first album. It was full of newspaper clippings. She nudged the book over on the tray. Lexi gasped.

Ursula said softly, "Some say the Holocaust never happened. They say the Jews made up the Holocaust so that we would feel sorry for them." She flipped the page. More skeletal faces stared out at them, rags barely covering their emaciated bodies. And not just men— women and children, too. "No one could make up lies like these."

Lexi reached out and turned the next page. "What's that?"

"Dead bodies," Ursula answered. "The Nazis killed

as fast as they could and threw the bodies into these mass graves." She turned the next page. "These photos were in papers all over the world after the war. No one could believe what had been going on. The destruction. The slaughter and executions." Her voice caught. She hated these pictures. But even more, she hated that there were those out there who didn't believe that it had ever happened.

Lexi opened the next album and slowly looked through all the clippings. Then the next and the next. The photos and articles covered all the years from the end of the war until the present day. Whenever Ursula had found a story about the Holocaust, she had clipped it and put it in the album.

Ursula pointed to a picture of an old woman that had an inset photo of a beautiful young woman. "That's what she looked like before the war. This is a story about a woman who lived in the forest for three years. She gave her baby to a Gentile family because she couldn't take care of it. She never saw her child again. And here's a story about a man who even to this day keeps bread in his pocket for fear of being without food. And this woman tells the story about some nuns who hid her from the Nazis, after she watched her mother and father and two little brothers dragged away from her."

They looked at the rest of the albums in silence. Lexi read all the captions and paused to read a few of the articles.

"Do you think this is all a lie?" Ursula asked gently.

Lexi looked at her with wide eyes and shook her head.

"Then why do you hang out with those who do?"

Lexi tensed. "They're my friends."

"But you're nothing like them," Ursula said, closing the last album.

"They're my family," Lexi protested. "They care about me."

Ursula shook her head. "They don't care about anyone. They're hard and ruthless. You still have heart and soul. I can see it in your eyes. It's not too late for you."

Lexi jumped up, knocking over her chair. "They do too care about me! More than my own family. My mom just cares about her booze, and my dad cares so much he dumped us all and took off for Switzerland," Lexi said harshly.

"It's true that families fall apart," Ursula conceded. "But you once had love holding you together, and that love is still there. You just have to believe that it can happen again in your life. On the other hand, what binds you to your Nazi friends is hate, the weakest kind of glue."

Lexi glared at her. "Just because you failed as a Nazi doesn't mean we will."

Ursula shook her head sadly. "I didn't fail as a Nazi. I failed as a human being." She closed her eyes and prayed for the memories to go away.

A moment later, she heard the heavy clomp of boots cross the floor as Lexi let herself out.

CHAPTER TEN

LEXI BURNED WITH ANGER as she hurried down the street. What did that old lady know about friendship? They *were* like family. They *were*.

She cut through people's backyards, heading toward Devon's house. That's where they hung out on Wednesdays and Fridays because on those days his mom worked. Devon had told her he never knew his dad.

She entered through the outside basement door as they all did.

Loud, crashing *oi* music pounded against her eardrums. The heavy rhythms thumped in her chest. She liked the neo-Nazi music, but she always felt slightly deaf after one of these sessions. And the one time she'd gone to a concert, she thought she'd lose her hearing permanently.

A black light glowed in the windowless room, and the choking thickness of tobacco smoke filled the air. A case of beer had been opened, half of it gone already. But then, her friends hadn't gone to school. They were either too old or had dropped out. In fact, she was the only one still in school.

Everyone was there. Karen was sitting by herself on the sagging couch, looking bored, a beer bottle dangling between two skinny fingers. She'd changed her nose hoop for a diamond stud that twinkled even in the dim light.

Billy and Devon were shooting darts, half the time missing the target entirely. The wall was pitted with holes.

In the corner, Mick and Serge were arguing. The music was too loud for her to hear anything, but it was obvious they were fighting about something.

Devon grinned when he caught sight of her, his teeth glowing slightly blue under the black light. "We're getting psyched up for tomorrow night," he yelled next to her ear, his booze breath fanning her cheek.

She nodded and saluted him. The shouting in the corner suddenly got louder, or maybe it only seemed louder with the lull in the music, the deep voice reciting the lyrics: "Come with me, come with me, we will be free of unity. One nation strong, so come along, but only white allowed!"

Mick put his hands on his hips and scowled, but Serge didn't back down. Instead, he stepped forward. Lexi couldn't make out what they were saying. Suddenly, Serge picked up the baseball bat leaning in the corner. He swung it at Mick's head.

Karen screamed but didn't move.

Mick ducked and reached out to grab the bat, but he missed. Serge reached back to swing again. On his back swing, he smashed the bat into the dual cassette boom box. It shattered, making a silence loud and sudden.

"I'm going to kill you!" Serge screamed, waving the bat wildly.

"Put that down!" Mick shouted. "I'm the leader! You have to do it my way!"

Serge advanced with the bat. "Your way is stupid. I can't believe you call yourselves Nazis."

Billy whispered in Lexi's ear, "They're talking about tomorrow night. They've been arguing about this all day."

Serge swung the bat again. This time, Mick charged as soon as the bat was out of the way. He tackled Serge and threw him to the ground. After some furious wrestling, Mick finally pinned Serge's squirming body on the beer-stained carpet. Serge was strong, but Mick had about thirty pounds on him. Thirty pounds of muscle.

"It's my plan, and we'll do it my way," Mick gasped.

Serge stopped struggling. He just stared up at Mick, his eyes flat and cold. "Your plan, maybe, but it was my idea in the first place! If it wasn't for me, you'd still be playing around spraypainting. The Jews think you're a bunch of punk kids, and you are. If you really want to scare them away, you have to do it my way."

"You done?" Mick asked.

Serge nodded curtly, but he didn't say anything. When Mick released him, he jumped to his feet. "You can do it your way if you want," Serge said, his voice filled with hatred. "But it won't do no good. You'll see. You'll need my plan to make it work." He glared around at the rest of them, giving Lexi an especially dirty look. With that, he stomped out of the basement, slamming the door behind him.

Mick picked up the fallen baseball bat and smashed it into the wall. It left a deep dent, cracks radiating out from it, jagging up the painted Sheetrock. He looked around. "What are you all staring at?" he demanded. "Just remember, tomorrow night you do what *I* say." He took Karen's arm and they left.

Billy slid out after them.

Lexi slumped onto the couch. It smelled like beer and was pocked with cigarette burns. What was happening to the Pack? She had just told Ursula what a great family they were, and here they were fighting and yelling at each other.

This was all Serge's fault, she decided. Before he came with his big ideas, they were happy just hanging out together, listening to music, and spraypainting stuff. So what if it was small time? That didn't mean they weren't good Nazis, whatever that meant.

She sighed. After reading Ursula's scrapbook, she didn't know what anything meant.

Devon sat down next to her.

She pointed to the smashed tape deck. "Bummer."

He shrugged. "It was Mick's."

She pointed to the bat mark on the wall. "Will your mom kill you?"

"Nah, she doesn't even come down here anymore. She don't care."

"Oh."

Without the *oi* music pounding in the background, without a fire to stare into, there didn't seem to be much to do or talk about.

"Want some munchies?" Devon asked.

"Sure."

"I'll get some." With that, he slipped upstairs.

Lexi looked around. The basement was divided into three parts. One part hid the furnace behind folding doors. The second section was the largest, where they hung out. And back in the corner was a door that she knew led to Devon's room, even though she'd never been back there.

Curious, she got up and opened his door, which he'd painted black, and flicked the switch on the wall. Another black light glowed from the ceiling. The room was small and square. On the wall over his unmade bed, he'd hung a hand-painted Nazi flag. The white around the black swastika glowed and looked really cool. Off to the right side, a table leaned against the wall, one leg missing. Lexi smiled wryly, wondering if Devon realized his table wasn't a good Nazi table: It was deformed.

She wandered over to it, flipping up the top of a box that was the only thing there. She rifled through it, but it was only filled with papers and beer bottle labels and a couple of photos. She heard Devon thumping down the stairs and was about to close the box when an old photo caught her eye. She picked it up and was staring at it when Devon came in.

"What are you doing?" He threw a bag of chips on his bed and grabbed the photo out of her hand. "Who said you could come in here?"

"I'm sorry," Lexi said. "I was just looking around. I didn't think you'd mind."

"Well, I do," Devon snapped. He hesitated a second, then, after a quick look at the photo, ripped it to shreds.

Lexi had never seen him so angry. "Who was that?"

Devon didn't answer. Little bits of the picture flaked to the floor like confetti at a celebration, only this didn't feel like a celebration.

"Who was that?" she asked again. Even though the photo was gone, she could still picture the man who had stared out at her. He stood tall and thin, wearing a heavy coat, dark slacks, and rubbers on his shoes. He looked like a geek. He also looked black. He had light skin, but his dark hair kinked.

She looked at Devon. She realized how much he looked like the man in the photo.

Devon must have seen the thought in her eyes because he suddenly sat on his bed and buried his face in his hands.

"That was your dad," Lexi said softly. "He's black, so you are, too."

"You can't prove it," Devon said, his voice muffled by his hands.

"Why do you hate blacks so much if you're part black, too?"

Devon jumped to his feet like a jack-in-the-box springing upward.

Startled, Lexi took a step back.

"Why?" he shouted. "Because my father left my mom as soon as he found out she was pregnant with me. I hate him! I disown him." He sliced his hand through the air. "I'm not a part of him, do you hear? I'm no nigger! And you can't prove that I am."

"I don't care," Lexi protested. "I don't care that you're part black. No one would really care."

Devon stared at her open-mouthed. "Are you kidding? If Serge and Mick found out, they'd *kill* me. You can't tell them."

"I won't, I won't, but I know they wouldn't *really* kill you. That's crazy. I mean, all that stuff about niggers and kikes and gooks. It's just talk."

Devon shook his head. "You don't get it, do you."

Lexi edged closer to the door. "Get what?"

"This whole Nazi skinhead stuff."

"I do, too." Lexi backed out of the room.

"If you did, you would hate me right now." His voice was quieter.

"I don't hate you."

Devon sighed. "I know, but you should." When Lexi opened her mouth to say something, he held up his hand. "Forget it. Just don't say anything to anyone, okay?"

Lexi nodded. "Why would I? We're family, right?"

Devon nodded, but he didn't look too certain. "Yeah," he agreed softly.

"I have to go," Lexi said. "I promised Shelby I'd do something with her today." She walked to the hatchway, pulling her hood up over her shaved head. "Don't worry, I won't say anything about . . . about your dad."

He nodded. Then he snapped his heels together and saluted her with a stiff arm. *"Heil Hitler!"*

CHAPTER ELEVEN

Quickly, Lexi walked out of the Flats and into the Heights. After Serge had moved here and found out where she lived, he didn't want her to stay in the Pack. He said that skins represented the working-class white race, and she was rich, but Mick said she could hang out with them. He said it didn't matter how much money her father made, since none of it was hers anyway.

Her neighborhood was called the Heights not only because it was a snobby reference to the fact that people living there had more money, more house, more prestige than those in the Flats, but because of the stupid hills, and she lived on one of the highest. By the time she got to the bottom of her road, her feet ached and she felt sweaty despite the cool air. It was a good thing she had three sweatshirts so she could dump this one in the wash when she got home and use her other one to hide her head from her mother.

As she trudged up the hill to her house, she walked

bent over like an old lady, trying to ignore the stabbing pain in her heel.

She rounded the final curve to her house and stopped dead. Two police cars were parked in her driveway. Her heart started to jackhammer. Shelby? Had something happened to her? Or had her mother fallen down the stairs after one too many drinks?

Lexi charged forward. She arrived at the side door gasping for breath. As soon as she burst into the house, she knew immediately she had been wrong. The police weren't there because something had happened to Shelby, and her mother hadn't taken a dive down the stairs. All eyes turned on her as she came into the kitchen.

"Where have you been?" her mother asked, stalking forward.

Immediately, Lexi's defenses went up. "Out."

Her mother waved toward the police officers. "They said you made a 911 call two nights ago. I told them that was impossible."

Lexi eyed the two officers. Pigs, Serge called them. One of them was black as burnt toast. Nigger, Devon would call him. The other one was a mixture of races. Scum, Billy would call him. Nigger scum pigs. But she couldn't help remembering the tender way a black policeman had held Nanna's hand until the paramedics came after her heart attack. And she had seen tears in his eyes. Did pigs cry?

"Lexi?" the black officer said.

Lexi stared stonily at him, hoping he didn't notice her quivering legs.

"We traced a 911 call to your phone," he glanced at his notepad, "at 11:34 Monday night. You reported an accident on Parker Street."

"So?"

"So?" her mother repeated. "Did you make the call, Alexandra?" She surged forward, her fists clenched as though to strike. "What's gotten into you, making crank calls? I'm taking that phone away from you this instant. And that's just the beginning!"

"Mrs. Jordan," the other officer interrupted, placing a hand on her shoulder. "It wasn't a prank. There really was a woman in need of help. The 911 call very well may have saved her life."

"What are you saying?" Lexi's mother demanded.

Both officers turned to Lexi. "How did you know Mrs. Zeidler needed help?"

Lexi glanced at her mother and then down at the floor. "I . . . I was walking by and I heard her cry out. So later I just thought I should, you know, report it in case she needed help."

For a very long moment no one said anything. Then one of the officers cleared his throat. "That's pretty much what Mrs. Zeidler said."

Lexi jerked her head up. "It is?"

"That's right."

"Oh." Lexi looked at the floor again. The police had questioned Ursula, but she hadn't reported her. Why had she protected her?

"But there is another matter we need to discuss with you. We wouldn't have even traced the call after hearing Mrs. Zeidler's story, except there were other reports of a kid in the area after the spraying of Temple Beth El. Know anything about that?"

Lexi shook her head.

He picked up a dark sweatshirt from the counter behind him. He pointed to the red paint. "Are you sure? Your mother let us look through your room before you got home, and we found this. Can you tell us why you have paint on your sweatshirt?"

Lexi glared at her mother. What right did she have letting these cops search her room? "That was from a project at school."

The black officer narrowed his eyes. "Are you sure it's not from spraypainting the synagogue Monday night?"

Mrs. Jordan gasped. "Are you insane? My daughter would never do that."

"Who else did it with you?"

"She couldn't have done that. Lexi, tell them!"

"If you give us some other names, we'll go lighter on you."

"But this is absurd. Lexi wouldn't deface a synagogue."

"We have witnesses who chased someone fitting your daughter's description. We believe she is the one."

"Lexi, tell them!"

Lexi opened her mouth. "I . . . I . . ."

"I can't believe it!" her mother burst out, grabbing Lexi's shoulders and shaking her. "You *did* do it! It's those animals you hang out with. Those worthless kids who have nothing better to do than hang around and cause problems." Her mother ranted on. "I forbid you to see them anymore. You stay home with your family, where you belong."

Lexi jerked out of her mother's grip and snorted. "Family? What family? So I can watch you get drunk every day? And flirt with those creeps you bring home? There's no family here except Shelby. My friends care about me. They are more my family than you!" With those words, she shoved back her hood.

Her mother pressed a hand to her mouth, staring at the crude swastika on Lexi's scalp. "Oh, no," she whimpered. "Oh, no."

"Mrs. Jordan," one of the officers said, "we're going to have to take your daughter down to the station for further questioning in this matter. You'd better follow in your car so you can drive her home."

"Is she . . . is she being arrested?"

"Not yet, but it's a good possibility."

The next day, Thursday, as soon as school was dismissed, Lexi practically ran to Ursula's house. The police had put her on a curfew, and she had to go home right after school, but first she had to talk to the old woman.

Out of breath, she rang the doorbell until the nurse with the white teeth let her in. Lexi avoided looking her in the eyes. It was almost as though the nurse had x-ray vision and could see under her hood and into her heart. Quickly, Lexi brushed by her.

Ursula's head was propped up and she smiled when she saw Lexi. "You look different," she said.

Lexi glanced down at herself. She had on sneakers and jeans, only these weren't so tight and rolled up at the ankles. She still wore a hooded sweatshirt to cover her head, but over it she wore a peach and mauve suede jacket. Her mother had thrown away all her black clothes and her Doc Martens, not that she was sorry to see those blistermakers go.

"How do you feel?" Lexi asked.

"Better. But it's going to take time to heal this old hip of mine."

Lexi shifted her book bag from one shoulder to the other. She couldn't remember the last time she'd brought books home, but it was one of the new rules until her court date.

"You look like you're in a hurry. Are you going to meet your . . . friends?"

Lexi blushed. Well, they were her friends. She hadn't ratted on them to the police. They were like family, and family stuck up for each other, right?

"No," Lexi said. "I just want to know why you didn't tell on me. The police came to my house yesterday. They said you told them you fell and I must have heard you from outside. Why didn't you tell them that it was all my fault you broke your hip?"

Ursula shook her head slowly. "Once upon a time, many years ago," she said softly, "I told on someone when I was sure it was the right thing to do, but it was horribly wrong."

Lexi didn't understand. "But you saw that it was my fault. I brought those kids to you."

"I saw that you were sorry for what you did," Ursula said. "You are sorry, aren't you?"

"Oh, yes. I really am." Tears filled Lexi's eyes. She tried to blink them back, but they skittled down her cheeks before she could wipe them away with her sleeve.

"Then I don't judge you beyond that. I learned a long time ago that I am not a judge. I leave that up to God."

Lexi nodded. She would have to run home to make it by curfew time. "I have to go. But . . . but thank you." She dashed toward the door. "I'll come visit again." Then she flew out of the house and up the hills toward home.

CHAPTER TWELVE

URSULA CLOSED HER EYES. Her hip ached and even short visits tired her out. But it was worth it to see Amy. . . . She supposed she would always think of her as Amy rather than Lexi . . . to see Amy's tears. Like rain that cleansed the earth, she knew that God had given humans tears to cleanse the heart and soul.

Perhaps that's what she needed: More tears to wash away the memories that haunted her. But did she have enough tears left?

"There's one of them now," Hildegard said, not even whispering. She pointed across the street.

Ursula's heart stung when she saw Helen hurrying past on the other side of the road, her head down as though praying no one would notice her.

"Come," Hildegard said. "Let's get her."

Ursula hesitated. "But I know her. Knew her," she amended quickly.

"She's a Jewess. A despicable one. The enemy."

She knew what Hildegard said was all true, yet it was

hard to imagine Helen as a despicable enemy. Memories of the Sabbath dinner floated through her head like faint wisps of steam. And the games they had played as young children. And the secrets they had shared.

She shook herself. Those memories were wrong, she told herself firmly. Hitler had shown them all the truth about the Jews and their evil ways.

"Are you coming?" Hildegard asked as she started across the street.

Ursula followed her friend. They tagged along behind Helen, getting closer and closer with each step. Pretty soon, Hildegard was stepping on Helen's heels. Helen tried to walk faster, but Hildegard just laughed.

Ursula bit her lip, hurrying to keep up, but not close enough to step on Helen's heels herself.

Suddenly, Hildegard reached forward and pushed Helen. With a cry, Helen lurched forward, landing on her knees and hands.

"That's where you belong," Hildegard said with a scornful giggle.

Helen struggled to get up, but Hildegard used her foot to keep her down.

Ursula watched as Hitler's voice rang in her ears. How many times had she heard him on the radio telling her that Jews were evil and it was their fault Germany was poor and weak? And it was true. Ursula had seen for herself that as more Jews fled Germany, her beloved Fatherland had become stronger. After all, her own

father now had a job, and they were no longer cold and hungry.

Helen looked up at her, silently pleading with her eyes. Dark, evil eyes, Ursula thought. She stuck out her own foot, pushing down on Helen's back with it.

"You can go home now," she said with a kind-sounding voice, "but you must stay on your hands and knees the whole way!"

Hildegard looked at her with amazement, then she shouted with laughter. "What a perfect idea!"

Ursula smiled, wondering why she felt a little sick inside. It was a perfect idea. Keep the dirty Jews on the ground where they belonged.

Whimpering, Helen struggled forward over the uneven stones of the sidewalk. Ursula and Hildegard kept right behind her, kicking her if Helen slowed down. As the trio made its way down the street, people stopped to watch. Children laughed and ran circles around them until their parents pulled them away. Adults just stared, their faces stony. Ursula didn't know if they watched with approval or disapproval, but she didn't care, she told herself. Jews had to be taught their place no matter what.

With Helen on her hands and knees, the walk home became slower and slower. Finally, they reached the small house Helen now lived in with her parents and other relatives. Helen's house had burned in a fire some time ago. Served them right for being so rich and flaunting it all the time, Ursula thought.

"May I stand up now?" Helen whispered, her head bowed nearly to the ground.

"No," Hildegard said.

Ursula looked toward the door of the house, imagining the shame Helen must be feeling, and how embarrassing it would be for her relatives to see her like that.

"Let her get up," Ursula said.

"What?" Hildegard protested.

Ursula waved her hand as if it didn't matter. "Let her walk to her own door." Then she turned to Helen. "But every time you see us, we expect you to drop to your hands and knees. Do you understand?"

Helen barely nodded. Slowly she stood up, gingerly wiping her cut and reddened hands together.

Ursula stared at Helen's knees. The girl's skirt had torn and frayed on the stones, revealing dirty, bloody knees. Helen kept her head down, but Ursula could see the tears that streaked her pale, drawn cheeks.

A deep sob escaped from the depths of her soul. In grief, Ursula turned her head to allow the pillow to soak up the tears she couldn't hold back. So many years had passed, but the pain of her cruelty to Helen hadn't diminished one bit. And that wasn't even the worst of it, she remembered with despair as another sob welled up, threatening to choke her.

Lexi made it home and shut the door of her bedroom as the grandfather clock in the foyer struck three. She had just made curfew, not that her mom was home to notice. She was probably off with a *business associate*. She should have a curfew, too. A curfew to come home alone, sober.

Lexi flopped back on her bed and stared up at the bare ceiling. She remembered a time when her mother had been there when she got home from school. It had been Lexi's favorite part of the day. Cookies and milk with Mommy, telling her about how well she had done on the spelling test, or the winning kickball team. And Mommy clapping her hands with delight, kissing her and hugging her. . . .

Then things had started to change. Her father had gotten a bigger, better job. He was never around. And when Lexi came home in the afternoons, Mommy wasn't waiting with milk and cookies and kisses. She was in her room crying, or out shopping with friends.

Nanna had moved in, bubbling and laughing, filling the empty spaces so well that at first Lexi hardly noticed the changes in her mother. But after Nanna's fatal heart attack, her mother had gotten a job. That's when the drinking had started. Or at least, that's when Lexi became aware of it. And the boyfriends.

One day Lexi had noticed her father's business trip had lasted over a month. When she asked her mother about it, she found out they were getting divorced. "I thought you knew, dear," her mother had said, sipping her champagne.

"It's all your fault!" Lexi had blazed. "You drink too

much. And what are those guys doing here all the time? You're cheating on Daddy!"

Her mother's face had turned white, her lips pressed to a thin line. "Don't you ever talk to me like that, Alexandra. You don't know anything."

But Lexi's pain was too great to keep to herself. "You're a lush and a slut."

For a moment, silence sliced the air like a razor. Then her mother whipped her hand forward and hit Lexi across the cheek.

That was the first time.

Lexi folded her arms across her eyes, wishing her thoughts could have stayed back with the milk and cookies. But, no matter how hard she tried, she couldn't hang on to those happier days.

Shelby knocked on the door and then waltzed in, twirling around.

Lexi sat up and gasped when she saw her younger sister. She grabbed Shelby's arm. "What have you done? Mom's going to kill you!"

Shelby yanked out of Lexi's grip and rubbed her arm. "She didn't kill you. And I like it."

"But you look stupid with a bald head," Lexi said bluntly.

"Stupid?" Shelby's face started to turn red. "*You* have a bald head, and I didn't say *you* look stupid. I think it looks cool. I like it!"

"How did you get that swastika on your head?"

Shelby grinned. "I used a black marker, but I'm going to get a permanent tattoo just like you."

"But you're only ten, Shel," Lexi said more calmly. "You're too young to know what you're doing."

"I am not. You taught me the salute and that niggers and kikes and people like that are bad. I'm old enough to learn."

Lexi bit her lip. Why did everything she had said and thought suddenly sound stupid? "Shelby, maybe I was wrong. . . . I'm not saying I was, but I've been thinking lately . . ."

Shelby sneered at her. "You just don't want me to have any fun."

In shock, Lexi realized that she had said those exact words to her mother. "I do want you to have fun, but it's dangerous hanging out with those guys."

"You're jealous because you don't want to share your friends. Serge will like me, even though he doesn't like you."

"How do you know Serge?" Lexi demanded. Her friends had come by the house a couple of times, but never long enough for Shelby to do more than stare at them from the top of the stairs. "Tell me!"

Shelby just tossed her shaved head and crossed her arms. "I don't have to tell you anything." With that, she marched out of the room. For the first time, Lexi noticed that her little sister was wearing tight jeans rolled up at the ankles, boots that she had stained black, and a dark sweatshirt with a hood.

CHAPTER THIRTEEN

L EXI CLOSED HER BOOK OF short stories and
yawned. Her mother had come home a couple of
hours ago, but it was oddly quiet downstairs. And when
she'd looked out the window, there was no stranger's
car parked in the driveway.

She hadn't seen Shelby since their little scene. She
was probably sulking in her room or, if she were smart,
hiding from their mom.

Slipping off the bed, Lexi stepped out onto the landing, listening for any signs of life in the big house. When
Nanna and her father had both lived there, the place
had seemed smaller and cozier. But now, with just the
three of them, the house had grown huge and cold and
unfriendly.

Sniffling noises came from the living room.

Lexi tiptoed down the stairs and peeked around the
corner. Her mother looked up from the couch at that moment, her eyes red and teary. Lexi had seen her mother's
eyes like that many times. Too much booze did that;
hangovers did that, too. But this time her eyes looked

different, sad. And there was no half-empty bottle on the coffee table.

Her mother stared at Lexi's bald head, with its slight burr of hair from not shaving it for the past few days. Her head now reminded her of her father's cheeks on a Sunday morning after he hadn't shaved all weekend.

She started to edge back out of sight, but her mother motioned her forward. "Come sit with me a moment, Alexandra," she said.

Lexi slowly walked over to the couch and sat at the far end, out of striking distance. Her mother didn't have to be drunk to hit her.

Her mother wore a gray and lavender plaid flannel lounge suit. Her feet were tucked into pink slippers. She fingered a corner of the blanket that was draped over her lap. "God, why did you shave your head? You look like a skeleton, you know."

Lexi began to stand up, but her mother quickly said, "No, don't go."

Lexi hesitated.

"It's just that those kids you hang out with—"

"They're my friends," Lexi said stonily. "I can talk to *them*."

"You should have come to me if you needed someone to talk to."

Lexi threw her hands up. "How could I? You're never home, and when you are, you have some guy with you and you're drunk."

"You don't understand anything, Lexi. You don't know what it's like for me. But I've decided to quit drinking."

"You've said that before."

"This time I mean it. I'm really going to . . . try. It wouldn't hurt if you tried to help me. It isn't easy. I've been through so much."

"So have I. Where were you when I needed you?" Lexi said, hating the way her throat choked up.

Her mother's eyes welled with tears. "I know," she whispered. "I haven't been there for you lately—"

"Lately?" Lexi interrupted. "Try years."

Her mother nodded quickly. "I . . . I just didn't know what to do, after Nanna's death, and—"

Lexi shot her an accusing glare. "You were drinking before then."

"True."

"And cheating on Daddy."

"Lexi, believe me, things are not what you think—"

"You drove him out."

"No, I didn't—"

Lexi stood up. "Don't lie to me! You'll never change." But even as she said it, she remembered when their lives had been different. Her mother had changed once. For the worse. Could she change back again? Lexi hated herself for even wondering, for wishing. Wishes weren't worth a damn.

Her mother stood up, too. "Don't talk to me like that, Alexandra. I'm your mother."

Lexi sneered. "So?" She almost felt sorry when she saw the helpless expression on her mother's face.

"So, I . . . I love you."

Lexi didn't want to hear anymore. The words hurt too much. These last few years she would have done anything to hear her mother say those words to her. But now, she thought, it was too late.

She ran upstairs and into her room, slamming the door behind her. She glanced at her clock. 10 P.M. She tapped on the door between her room and her sister's, but Shelby didn't answer. Opening the door, she looked around. The pink-and-white room was empty.

An uneasy feeling crept up her back.

Then she remembered that the computer had been on when she got home. She pulled out her secret disk from its hiding spot. Inserting it, she clicked through the screens until she brought up her diary. She scrolled to the end. And then she knew. There was nothing written there, but Lexi knew that someone had been reading her diary, for that someone had inadvertently added an extra blank page, something Lexi never did.

No wonder Shel knew all about Serge. She read through her last entry.

Wednesday 9:10 P.M.

Well, we're finally back from the police station. The fingerprints on the can matched mine, so they know I sprayed the synagogue. But I didn't tell on anyone else. They couldn't make me.

I can't believe it. Devon is black—well, like part black. I'm not kidding. I saw this picture of his dad, and he nearly flipped out that I knew. He made me promise not to tell anyone. As if anyone would really care. I even tried to tell him that, but he acted all scared and stuff, so I won't tell. It's kind of weird that he's black, but he calls blacks "niggers" and seems to hate them more than anyone else. I don't get it.

Tomorrow is the big event. Big Tree, 10 P.M. I'm on curfew, though, so I won't be able to go. Serge will definitely use that as a reason to kick me out of the Pack. Maybe I'll sneak out. I don't know. Maybe I'll just stay home and read a book. Haven't done that in awhile.

Didn't hear from Daddy. So what else is new?

The uneasiness in her belly had become burning, churning acid, eating away at her insides like some kind of alien.

Without thinking, she grabbed her suede coat and stuffed her feet into a pair of sneakers. Without heavy boots on, it would be easier to slip out. She knew that she was breaking her curfew, but she had to find Shelby.

The cold air prickled the skin on her scalp, but she barely noticed as she ran down the hill, her arms pumping at her sides. For a moment she almost felt like she was up early, before dawn, jogging with her father. Just for a moment. Then the illusion disintegrated as the wail of a distant siren sliced through her thoughts like a knife through flesh.

She sprinted.

They were supposed to meet at the tree at 10. Were they still there? Did the sirens have anything to do with what the Pack was doing?

She veered in the direction that would take her to the Big Tree first, hoping, praying they were there, arguing about whose plan they would follow.

The woods were silent. She heard the sirens, now muffled by the trees, and with each wail, she grew more frightened.

She burst into the clearing, wildly looking around. Empty.

"Shelby?" she called anyway. "Shel? Are you here?"

There was silence, except for the skittering of some nighttime animal through the crackling underbrush.

And a gurgle.

Lexi froze, listening, straining to hear another sound. "Shel?"

Slowly, she turned a full circle, staring into the shadows, imagining shapes and forms undulating around her, like demons dancing in the dark. Then she really did see something move. A hand.

"Shelby!" She ran toward the body lying on the ground. The face was battered, and even in the dark she could see black smears that could only be blood. One eye was puffed completely closed. The breathing came in short, weak rasps.

Relief flooded through her. It wasn't Shelby.
Immediately she felt terrible for feeling so relieved.
"Devon, what happened to you?" she whispered.

He moaned softly, trying to catch his breath at the
same time. "You . . . ," he said weakly. "You . . . you
told."

Lexi gently took his right hand, the only part of his
body that didn't look torn and bruised. "Told what?"

"My father," he gasped, wincing as some internal pain shot through him.

"No, Devon!" she exclaimed as she realized what he was talking about. "I swore to you I wouldn't." Then horror seized her. "You mean, *they* did this to you? Mick and them?"

"Who do you think?"

She could barely hear his voice through the heavy thumping in her ears that sounded like hundreds of marching combat boots. The thumping of her heart.

"They wanted to kill me. Serge called me a nigger." A spasm shook his body.

"I didn't tell, I swear. I wouldn't do that to you." Tears spilled onto her cheeks, and she brushed them away. How could they have hurt their friend? Why? So what if he was part black? Did it really matter?

The knot in her stomach told her that yes, it did really matter. To them. Being a Nazi skinhead wasn't just a place to go to hang out with friends. They weren't a big happy family with relatives all over the country, all over the world. It wasn't a game to them.

"Did you tell your sister? Maybe she told them," he said, closing his one good eye.

Her heart felt as if it might stop. "Shel was here?" She looked around frantically. "Where is she?"

"Gone with them."

"To the synagogue?"

"Yeah," he gasped out. "Fire. Burn."

CHAPTER FOURTEEN

LEXI DROPPED DEVON'S HAND as though it had suddenly burst into flames, and it fell heavily as though it were attached to a dead person. She stumbled to her feet. "They have Shelby?"

Devon groaned.

"Oh no," she cried, but only a small sound, like that of a frightened animal, escaped her throat. "I'll send help for you, but I have to go find Shelby."

She raced away from the clearing, pushing through branches that clutched at her jacket and feet, trying to trip her, stop her. At last she reached the street and she opened up, flying down the sidewalk toward the synagogue. The event. The big plan.

She smelled the smoke three blocks away. She picked up speed, tearing around corners, cutting through backyards.

The flames from the burning building lit the whole square. She ran forward, pushing through the gathering crowd. People turned to stare at her, first in surprise, then with scorn and even hatred in their eyes. Someone dug an elbow deep into her ribs, someone else kicked her shins as she passed.

Lexi pushed on, jumping now and then to try to see beyond the crowd.

A woman grabbed her arm. "What are you doing here? Did you start this fire?"

Lexi tried to pull free. "I didn't do it. I'm looking for my sister."

"You little neo-Nazi, you're a devil." She practically spat at Lexi. "There are people trapped in there, caught in the fire!"

"No!" Lexi's knees buckled, but the woman's grip held her up.

The woman shoved her away. "You're a murdering Nazi like the rest of them."

Filled with fear, Lexi searched for Shelby. She couldn't be one of the ones caught in the fire.

She stumbled forward and cried with relief when she saw Billy sidling around the edges of the crowd, head low and covered by a ski cap.

"Billy!" she yelled.

His head jerked up. When he saw her, he moved faster, away from her.

She ran after him. "Where are you going?"

He ignored her and kept moving.

Finally she caught up to him and yanked on his arm. "What's going on? Have you seen Shelby? Are there really people caught inside?"

He didn't look at her.

"Answer me!"

When he turned to her, it was as if he didn't know her and didn't want to. "Let go of me," he growled. "You're an idiot to walk around like that." He motioned to her bare head.

"Where's my little sister? Have you seen her?"

He shook off her hand. "Yeah, I saw her. Haven't seen her since we started the fire."

"Help me look for her!"

"No way. The pigs are on the rampage. I'm out of here."

"But . . . but we're family." Even to her the words sounded lame.

He snorted. "Get real." Then he slipped into the crowd and disappeared from sight.

Lexi stood frozen. How could she have been so wrong about everything?

Was her sister in the burning synagogue? No, she refused to believe that. She would find Shelby in some hidden corner, safe and scared. Alive.

Frantic, she scanned the crowd. She recognized a round face and ran forward. The girl turned to her, first with a tremulous smile as she recognized Lexi, and then with shock as her gaze moved immediately to the tattoo.

Lexi grabbed Ellen's hand. Horror filled the girl's eyes, mixing with the reflection of the flames from the fire. Ellen pulled her hand free, and Lexi knew what she must have been thinking. But there was no time to worry about that now.

"I can't talk, but there's a boy who's hurt real bad in Crocker's Woods, near the Big Tree. Please, call the police or an ambulance. Send some help."

Ellen clutched Lexi's arm as Lexi started to move away. Tears streaked her cheeks. "Did you do this?"

Lexi shook her head fiercely. "No, I swear." Then she raised trembling fingers to the side of her scalp where she knew her swastika sat like a spider. "I can't explain now, but I will. Later. Please call about the boy. His name is Devon."

She heard a shout behind her. Whirling around, she spotted two policemen running toward her. With a gasp of fear, Lexi took off toward the burning synagogue. She ran as if she were at a track meet, dodging around people, elbowing through them if she couldn't get around them fast enough. She couldn't get caught. She had to find Shelby.

Ursula heard the sirens and she knew something had happened. Something big. Something terrible.

A feeling of dread overwhelmed her. She was sucked into a whirlpool of memories, and she couldn't swim out of it no matter how hard she tried. No matter how long she had been swimming. Sucked down and down.

Memories whirled in her brain, a vortex that drew her down, drowning her.

"There they are," Hildegard whispered.

Ursula stared out the window at the night scene, her heart thumping, mouth dry. Just this afternoon they had reported the Reinekes to their *Jungmädel* troop leader. She had praised them and told them she would forward their report right away.

Now Ursula watched as the Gestapo's truck, headlights glaring, pulled to the curb and four large men got out, their heavy, hobnailed boots clacking on the cobblestones, hurrying to the Reineke's door. The guns in their hands glinted in the headlights.

"Why are they ramming the door like that?" Ursula wondered out loud.

Hildegard nudged her. "They want to get in."

"Can't they knock?"

Before Hildegard could answer, the neighbor's door splintered under the assault and burst open. The four men disappeared inside.

"What are they doing?" Ursula asked.

"Searching the house for Jews," Hildegard said. "I hope they find some. Then we will be heroes."

"But they just barged in."

Hildegard laughed. "Do you think they should be polite to traitors? To the enemy?"

"But what if they aren't traitors? What if we were wrong?"

"Don't say that," Hildegard said. "I pray we are right. Don't you?"

Ursula couldn't say anything. She couldn't tell her friend that this terrifying scene wasn't what she had imagined.

"Then my parents will love me like they do Wolfgang," Hildegard continued.

Ursula barely heard her. She could only hear the sound of shouting coming from the house across the street. Lights now burned in every window, but the window under the eaves remained dark. She kept her eyes wide, afraid if she blinked she'd miss something. She stared hard until lights danced before her eyes. She had to blink. No, it wasn't her imagination, there were lights flashing behind the attic window. More lights.

A gunshot. The shouting stopped.

Ursula held her breath.

"They must have found someone," Hildegard said, her voice high with excitement.

Minutes later, two Gestapo agents emerged from the house across the street, dragging a limp body by the arms. Two prisoners followed close behind, huddled together, and behind them came two more, pushed and threatened by the remaining Gestapo officers. They all stepped into the glare of the truck headlights.

Ursula cried out.

It was almost as if they had heard her, for two pairs of dark eyes stared up at her in her window.

Tears warmed Ursula's cheeks as she watched Helen Gutemann and her mother shoved into the truck along

with the Reinekes. The limp body of Herr Gutemann,
the rabbi, was tossed into the back like a sack of grain.

The vehicle started with a cough and groan, as
though it didn't want to go where it was going, then it
veered away from the curb, racing down the street out
of sight, into the night.

The piercing wail of another siren brought Ursula
back to the present, and her memories faded.

What she had done to the Gutemanns so many years
ago was unforgivable, though she had been praying for
forgiveness ever since, and unforgettable, though she
had been trying desperately to forget. But she had never
truly forgotten. And now this young girl with the tattoo
on her scalp had come along and shattered the wall
she'd built up over the years. She remembered all too
well of whom the girl reminded her. Herself.

It was too late for her, but surely there was still time
for Lexi, time to understand and time to change before
the young girl did something unforgivable, unforgettable. Or was it too late? Had the deadly spider snared
yet another victim in its treacherous web?

CHAPTER FIFTEEN

THE POLICE CORNERED LEXI. They grabbed her roughly, pinning her arms at her side.

"Let me go!" she screamed, struggling to get free. "I have to find Shelby." They were so close to the burning building she could feel the heat of the fire flushing her cheeks.

"Calm down," an officer said.

Lexi struggled more. "I have to find my sister."

The cops looked over her head at each other with raised eyebrows. She didn't care what they were thinking. She had to get loose.

"We're going to have to cuff you," one of them said brusquely.

Lexi sobbed. "You can't. I have to find her. Please. My sister might be trapped in the fire."

"There are firefighters in there right now. If she's inside, they'll get her. Won't do you any good to get in more trouble with us."

"More trouble? But I didn't do anything." She

tugged against their hands that still held her. "I didn't do anything. Aren't you listening?"

"We just want to ask you some questions, Alexandra."

"How do you know my name? Why are you holding me? I want to find my sister!" Panic coiled inside her, threatening to explode. "Please, let me go."

"Alexandra!"

Lexi turned to see her mother rushing toward her.

"You called my mother?" she flared at one of the officers she recognized from yesterday. "But I didn't *do* anything."

As her mother reached her, Lexi stiffened, waiting for a blow. Nothing and nobody would stop her mother this time. "What have you done?" she screamed.

Lexi bit her lip. Why had she even hoped in a tiny part of her heart that her mother would be on her side? "I didn't do anything," she said through stiff lips. Why wasn't anyone listening to her? Didn't they care about Shelby? About the people caught inside the synagogue?

"Do you know how worried I was when I found you gone? I called the police right away. And where's your sister? The two of you are killing me. I—"

"Stop it," Lexi cried. "Just stop it. All you care about is *you*. What about *us?* Shel may be inside there! Do you care about that?"

Lexi had always thought her heart would someday turn to ice, a way to escape all the pain, a way not to feel, but suddenly she realized it had turned to ice a long time ago. Now, for some reason, in what felt like a flood, her heart seemed to melt in her chest and a terrible agony washed through her. All the hurt and anger she'd tried not to feel for the last few years pierced her.

With a cry that welled up like a tidal wave, growing in power and pain with every second, she wrenched herself free from the hands that restrained her and ran closer to the synagogue. Closer. The heat scorched her skin. A gaping, black hole had opened up on one side of the building where the timbers had already fallen in.

Lexi sidestepped the heavily suited men and women whose job it was to put out fires and save lives, and ran right for the hole. She felt the woosh of hands on her shoulders as people tried to grab her when they realized what she was doing, but she ducked and dodged and pulled free.

All she thought was that Shelby must be inside, and that she had to save her little sister. Shelby was the only real family she had left. She couldn't lose her.

Heat seared her face and scalp. Smoke choked her, squeezing her lungs like someone wringing a washcloth.

"Shelby!" she screamed.

The flames had died down in this area, but they gave light to a long passage. More fire glowed at the end of it, but it was the only clear way to go.

She stumbled along, looking into rooms off the main hall and calling her sister's name through fits of coughing.

Walls crashed at the end of the hall and sent smoke billowing toward her. Through tearing eyes, Lexi watched, waiting for the smoke to engulf her.

Then three huge figures appeared, charred black and walking stiffly like zombies. For a moment, Lexi thought perhaps she had died and the demons had come to claim her, but as the figures came closer, she saw that they were firefighters in heavy gear. Each of the three was carrying a limp body over his shoulder.

Lexi ran toward them. They motioned her away, back toward the entrance, but she had to see.

With smoke swirling around her, she looked at the bodies. The glint of a gold nose ring gave a hint of who the first one might be.

With a lurching stomach, Lexi looked at the next body. It was Serge. His hands flopped lifelessly. His face was badly burned, as though a shaft of fire had been aimed across his eyes like a Halloween mask.

And the third body. Shelby's.

They reached the exit to the burning building. Hands grabbed her, and someone shoved an oxygen mask against her face. She tried to fight, but her limbs refused to cooperate. Two of the three bodies that had been retrieved from the fire were laid out on stretchers. EMTs fussed over them, attaching IVs and rushing them toward the ambulances. One body remained.

"I'm fine," Shelby protested, coughing but refusing to stay down.

Lexi finally pushed away the hands restraining her and rushed to her sister. Shelby's bare head was puckered with blisters, and the swastika she had drawn on earlier was now only a faint smudge, like a distant memory.

"Are you okay?" Lexi choked out.

Shelby nodded, tears clearing paths over her soot-smeared cheeks. "I'm so sorry," she whispered.

Lexi took her sister in her arms, the way her mother used to embrace her, so long ago, cradling, rocking, making quiet noises in her throat as though that were enough to keep away the terrors of the world.

"This one's the lucky one," Lexi heard someone say. "Don't know if that other girl will make it, and the boy's blind for sure, but he'll live."

"Stupid kids, don't they have anything better to do?"

"Blame the parents. Kids are kids, and they don't know what they're doing. . . ." The voices melted into the blur of sounds surrounding her, and she hugged her sister even closer.

Did they know what they were doing? Serge did. And Mick. What about Karen and Billy and Devon? And what about herself and Shelby? What did they really know about what they were doing? Who was to blame?

When a gentle hand pressed her shoulder, she looked up, surprised to see her mother standing there awkwardly, like a stranger.

Lexi hesitated only a second, then opened her arms. Her mother fell into them and they all held each other close as though they were, once again, a family.

Laura E. Williams was born in Seoul, Korea. She has lived in Belgium, Hawaii, and, for a few months, on a sailboat on the Caribbean. In 1983 Laura graduated from Denison University, and in 1988 she graduated from Trinity College with an M.A. in literary writing. She also earned a masters in education degree from St. Joseph College. She is the author of *Behind the Bedroom Wall,* the 1996 winner of the Milkweed Prize for Children's Literature, and *The Long Silk Strand* (Boyds Mills). She currently resides in Ohio.

Interior design by Donna Burch
Typeset in Sabon
by Stanton Publication Services, Inc.
Printed on acid-free 55# Sebago Antique cream paper
by Maple-Vail Book Manufacturing

If you enjoyed this book, you will also want to read these other Milkweed novels:

Gildaen, The Heroic Adventures of a Most Unusual Rabbit
by Emilie Buchwald

Chicago Tribune Book Festival Award, Best Book for Ages 9–12

Gildaen is befriended by a mysterious being who has lost his memory but not the ability to change shape at will. Together they accept the perilous task of thwarting the evil sorcerer, Grimald, in this tale of magic, villainy, and heroism.

No Place
by Kay Haugaard

Arturo Morales and his fellow sixth-grade classmates decide to improve their neighborhood and their lives by building a park in their otherwise concrete, inner-city Los Angeles barrio. The kids are challenged by their teachers to figure out what it would take to transform the neighborhood junkyard into a clean, safe place for children to play. Despite their parents' skepticism and the threat of street gangs, Arturo and his classmates struggle to prove that the actions of individuals—even kids—can make a difference.

The Gumma Wars
by David Haynes

Larry "Lu" Underwood and his fellow West 7th Wildcats have been looking forward to Tony Rodriguez's birthday fiesta all year—only to discover that Lu must also spend the day with his two feuding "gummas," the name he gave his grandmothers when he was just learning to talk. The two "gummas," Gumma Jackson and Gumma Underwood, are hostile to one another, especially when it comes to claiming the affection of their only grandson. On the action-packed day of Tony's birthday, Lu, a friend, and the gummas find themselves exploring the sights of Minneapolis and St. Paul—and eventually find themselves enjoying each other's company.

Business As Usual
by David Haynes

In Mr. Harrison's sixth-grade class, the West 7th Wildcats must learn how to run a business. Kevin Olsen, one of the Wildcats as well as the class clown, is forced out of the Wildcat group and into an unwilling alliance working in a group with the Wildcats' nemesis, Jenny Pederson. In the process of making staggering amounts of cookies for Marketplace Day, the classmates venture into the realm of free enterprise, discovering more than they imagined about business, the world, and themselves.

The Monkey Thief
by Aileen Kilgore Henderson

New York Public Library Best Books of the Year: "Books for the Teen Age"

Twelve-year-old Steve Hanson is sent to Costa Rica for eight months to live with his uncle. There he discovers a world completely unlike anything he can see from the cushions of his couch back home, a world filled with giant trees and insects, mysterious sounds, and the constant companionship of monkeys swinging in the branches overhead. When Steve hatches a plan to capture a monkey for himself, his quest for a pet leads him into dangerous territory. It takes all of Steve's survival skills—and the help of his new friends—to get him out of trouble.

The Summer of the Bonepile Monster
by Aileen Kilgore Henderson

Milkweed Prize for Children's Literature

Alabama Library Association 1996 Juvenile/Young Adult Award

Eleven-year-old Hollis Orr has been sent to spend the summer with Grancy, his father's grandmother, in rural Dolliver, Alabama, while his parents "work things out." As summer begins, Hollis encounters a road called Bonepile Hollow, barred by a gate and a real skull and bones mounted on a board. "Things that go down that road don't ever come back," he is told. Thus begins the mystery that plunges Hollis into real danger.

Treasure of Panther Peak
by Aileen Kilgore Henderson

Twelve-year-old Page Williams begrudgingly accompanies her mother, Ellie, as she flees her abusive husband, Page's father. Together they settle in a fantastic new world — Big Bend National Park, Texas. Wild animals stalk through the park, and the nearby Ghost Mountains are filled with legends of lost treasures. As Page tests her limits by sneaking into forbidden canyons, Ellie struggles to win the trust of other parents. Only through their new-found courage are they able to discover a treasure beyond what they could have imagined.

I Am Lavina Cumming
by Susan Lowell

Mountains & Plains Booksellers Association Award

In 1905, ten-year-old Lavina is sent from her home on the Bosque Ranch in Arizona Territory to live with her aunt in the city of Santa Cruz, California. Armed with the Cumming family motto, "courage," Lavina deals with a new school, homesickness, a very spoiled cousin, an earthquake, and a big decision about her future.

The Boy with Paper Wings
by Susan Lowell

Confined to bed with a viral fever, eleven-year-old Paul sails a paper airplane into his closet and propels himself into mysterious and dangerous realms in this exciting and fantastical adventure. Paul finds himself trapped in the military diorama on his closet floor, out to stop the evil commander, KRON. Armed only with paper and the knowledge of how to fold it, Paul uses his imagination and courage to find his way out of dilemmas and disasters.

The Secret of the Ruby Ring
by Yvonne MacGrory

Winner of Ireland's Bisto "Book of the Year" Award

Lucy gets a very special birthday present, a star ruby ring, from her grandmother and finds herself transported to Langley Castle in the Ireland of 1885. At first, she is intrigued by castle life, in which she is the lowliest servant, until she loses the ruby ring and her only way home.

A Bride for Anna's Papa
by Isabel R. Marvin

Milkweed Prize for Children's Literature

Life on Minnesota's iron range in 1907 is not easy for thirteen-year-old Anna Kallio. Her mother's death has left Anna to take care of the house, her young brother, and her father, a black-smith in the dangerous iron mines. So she and her brother plot to find their father a new wife, even attempting to arrange a match with one of the "mail order" brides arriving from Finland.

Minnie
by Annie M. G. Schmidt

Winner of the Netherlands' Silver Pencil Prize as One of the Best Books of the Year

Miss Minnie is a cat. Or rather, she *was* a cat. She is now a human, and she's not at all happy to be one. As Minnie tries to find and reverse the cause of her transformation, she brings her reporter friend, Mr. Tibbs, news from the cats' gossip hotline—including revealing information that one of the town's most prominent citizens is not the animal lover he appears to be.

The Dog with Golden Eyes
by Frances Wilbur

Milkweed Prize for Children's Literature

Many girls dream of owning a dog of their own, but Cassie's wish for one takes an unexpected turn in this contemporary tale of friendship and growing up. Thirteen-year-old Cassie is lonely, bored, and feeling friendless when a large, beautiful dog appears one day in her suburban backyard. Cassie wants to adopt the dog, but as she learns more about him, she realizes that she is, in fact, caring for a full-grown Arctic wolf. As she attempts to protect the wolf from urban dangers, Cassie discovers that she possesses strengths and resources she never imagined.

Behind the Bedroom Wall
by Laura E. Williams

Milkweed Prize for Children's Literature

It is 1942. Thirteen-year-old Korinna Rehme is an active member of her local *Jungmädel,* a Nazi youth group, along with many of her friends. Korinna's parents, however, secretly are members of an underground group providing a means of escape to the Jews of their city and are, in fact, hiding a refugee family behind the wall of Korinna's bedroom. As Korinna comes to know the family, and their young daughter, her sympathies begin to turn. But when someone tips off the Gestapo, loyalties are put to the test and Korinna must decide in what she believes and whom she trusts.

Milkweed Editions publishes with the intention of making a humane impact on society, in the belief that literature is a transformative art uniquely able to convey the essential experiences of the human heart and spirit.

To that end, Milkweed publishes distinctive voices of literary merit in handsomely designed, visually dynamic books, exploring the ethical, cultural, and esthetic issues that free societies need continually to address.

Milkweed Editions is a not-for-profit press.